WICKED IN WINTER

THE WICKED WINTERS BOOK 1

SCARLETT SCOTT

Happily Ever After Books

Wicked in Winter

The Wicked Winters Book 1

All rights reserved.

Copyright © 2019 by Scarlett Scott

Published by Happily Ever After Books, LLC

Edited by Grace Bradley

Cover Design by Wicked Smart Designs

For more information, contact author Scarlett Scott.

www.scarlettscottauthor.com

For my mother. Again. Just don't read it, Mom.

CHAPTER 1

LONDON, 1813

*L*ady Emilia King handed off her gloves and hat as she returned home from paying calls, scarcely suppressing a sigh. Her acquaintances were leaving her behind, and though she did not regret the decision to remain unwed, inwardly, she could admit to a small sliver of envy. Most of her friends were marrying or married, and some of them had already become mothers twice and thrice over.

As she crossed the familiar marble of the entryway, met by the forbidding oil relics owned by a succession of Dukes of Abingdon before Papa, she knew the familiar comfort of returning home.

Mama appeared suddenly before her then, her countenance troubled.

"*He* is here, Emilia," she warned in a tortured whisper.

Emilia's comfort was promptly dashed. In its place was a sickening swirl of dread and loathing. She knew the identity of their unwanted visitor without asking.

"What is he doing here again?" she asked. "This is the third time in as many days."

"He wishes to see you." Mama spoke *sotto voce*, but there was an unmistakable tremor in her voice. "He refuses to leave until he has had an audience, and Abingdon says you must, Emilia."

Emilia's heart ached at her mother's revelation, not just because she had no wish to meet the scoundrel who had appeared, once more, demanding to usurp her time. But also because the old Papa would not have required her to lower herself by remaining in the presence of such an unsuitable cur. Papa, before his illness, had been a bastion of propriety and elegance. He had been a proud man, descended from a noble line of dukes, always above reproach.

"I will not meet him," she denied quietly. "I fear I have a megrim, and I must seek my chamber at once."

Her trusted lady's maid, Redmayne, followed discreetly behind them as she sailed past her distraught mother. She knew Redmayne would never speak a word of this below stairs, but neither did she care for an audience.

"Emilia," Mama called after her, a stern note of censure entering her voice. "I am afraid we haven't a choice."

Emilia stopped. A chill settled over her, and it had nothing to do with the dampness of the autumn air and everything to do with Mama's choice of words. She turned back to her mother, attempting to calm herself.

"*We* haven't a choice?" she asked.

"None of us," Mama repeated, her tone mournful. "I… would you excuse us please, Redmayne?"

Her mother's sudden dismissal of her lady's maid only served to heighten the chill. "Mama?"

Redmayne curtseyed and quietly took her leave.

Mama stepped forward, clasping her hands. "Forgive me, Emilia. I have failed you."

"Mama?" A wild sense of panic descended. Instinctively,

she tightened her grip upon her mother. "What are you saying? You are frightening me."

"Abingdon has lost nearly everything," Mama revealed. "He has been wagering, quite heavily, it would seem. I had not realized the full extent of it until today."

"Papa has been gambling?" she asked, shock making her tongue go dry. "How can it be? He has never indulged in vice."

A tear tracked down Mama's cheek before she released Emilia's hands and dashed it away. "He has since his…illness."

Dear God.

She struggled to comprehend. One moment, she had been returning from something as commonplace as her daily calls, and the next, she was being bombarded. "I do not understand, Mama. What has Papa's infirmity and his sudden desire to gamble have to do with that dreadful man?"

She refused to speak his name. Thinking of him was painful enough. He was too broad, too coarse, too common.

Too handsome, reminded a voice inside herself.

One she banished with haste.

"Lady Emilia," said a smooth, deep voice behind her.

His voice.

She spun about, her last impression of Mama's horrified face instantly replaced by the hulking beast before her. He was tall, harsh, and brawny. He was not thin and elegant, not artfully dressed, not pleasant in mannerisms or gallant in gesture as gentlemen ought to be. As James had been. But James had been a lord, the son of an earl, a viscount in his own right.

This man was the furthest one could get from noble.

He was immense, his chest as sturdy as a wall, his thighs like the trunks of two trees. His raven hair fell in unruly waves, brushing his shoulders. He wore a plain black coat, buff trousers, and a matching waistcoat. His cravat was tied in a simple knot. Everything about him bespoke his background.

He was someone she ought not to know, her inferior in every way.

"Mr. Winter," she bit out coldly, as if his very name were an epithet.

And it may as well have been, for the man had been tormenting her ever since he had claimed the home next door to her father's townhome three years prior. He was surly. Ill-mannered. Grasping.

And beautiful.

Nay. Not beautiful. He was scandalous. Mr. Devereaux Winter was the darling of every scandal sheet in London. Polite society scorned him, as they should. If common fame was to be believed, Mr. Winter delighted in hosting ribald parties, parading a bevy of the most beautiful lightskirts in London about town, dueling, and brawling. He was rough, uncouth, and rich as Croesus.

"My lady," he said formally, sketching a passable bow.

"Why have you come?" she asked, unimpressed by his attempt.

"To collect my debt." His expression was devoid of emotion.

Behind her, Mama began sobbing quietly.

Emilia's breath caught. "I beg your pardon?"

Surely this owner of factories and tenements, this lowborn rascal, could not be implying what she thought he was. Mama's earlier words mingled with his terse statement to send a swirl of worry and fear churning through her.

"I did not misspeak." He remained aloof, unsmiling. "Perhaps you would deign to have an audience with me now, my lady."

"No," she denied without hesitation. "I will not."

4

"You misunderstand me, Lady Emilia." His voice was cold. "I was not making a request, but rather a command."

She bristled, throwing back her shoulders and tipping up her chin. Defiance snapped through her. "I am not yours to command, Mr. Winter."

For the first time, a small smile played about the corners of his lips. "How wrong you are, my lady. I am afraid I own you, this house, and everything within it."

Mama gasped behind her. "Mr. Winter, please, I beg you, do not make a scene."

Something inside Emilia froze. It was not hope, for that had been dashed long ago with James's death. Whatever the nameless emotion was, it withered and died in that moment, like a rose left on the bush after winter's first frost. Wilted. Crumpled.

Gone.

She wanted to turn back to her mother, to demand an explanation, but along with the cold leaching into the very marrow of her bones now came an understanding. A life-altering event had occurred, and the man before her was the source of that indefinable incident.

Mr. Winter held out his hand to her. "Lady Emilia, come with me, and I shall explain everything."

Her instinct told her he was a dangerous man. That placing her hand in his, and following him anywhere, would be a mistake. James's pale, golden looks, gorgeous manners, and courtly nature could not be further from this brute.

She remained stalwart, refusing to accept his gesture. "I do not wish to hear your explanation, Mr. Winter. If you will excuse me, I fear I am suffering from a dreadful megrim, and it has brought me home from my social calls earlier than anticipated. I cannot bear to stand here tarrying a moment more."

In your insufferable presence, she may have added, but she did not.

Instead, she met his gaze, resolute, daring him to call her a liar.

"You are lying, Lady Emilia," he pronounced without hesitation.

The devil.

She could not restrain her gasp at his audacity. "How dare you cast aspersions upon my character, Mr. Winter, when you have inveigled your way into my home, unexpected, unannounced, and dare to make demands upon my time? Demands you have no right to claim, I may add."

Mama moved forward, appearing at Emilia's side. She clutched at Emilia's elbow, her grasp desperate, akin to a woman clinging to the shore lest she be swept away in the raging swell of a flooded river.

"Emilia," she chided softly. "Please."

It was her mother's request, the pleading in her tone, the desperation she could not help but to sense, that forced her, at long last, to relent. Whatever dreadful thing had happened, there was a possibility Emilia's continued resistance would only serve to make it worse, and she had no desire to cause further upset for Mama and Papa. They had already endured so much on account of Papa's infirmity.

A knot of apprehension coiled within her as she looked to her mother. "You would have me meet with this man?" she asked.

Mama cast her eyes downward. "You must."

"Alone?" she persisted, knowing without hearing Mama's reply what the answer was. Knowing also what that answer meant for her.

"Yes," Mama whispered, still refusing to meet her gaze.

Dear God.

There was only one conclusion to be reached by such a

grim revelation. Somehow, some way, they had been ruined by the dastardly Mr. Winter. And so, in turn, would she be.

"Lady Emilia," the villain persisted then, his voice a gruff, low growl that was at once smooth yet hard. One part blade, one part velvet. "Come with me now."

She shrugged free of her mother's grasp, moving forward with the dour determination of a woman facing the gallows for a crime she had not committed. "Very well, Mr. Winter. It would seem you have won."

And with each step that carried her closer to a private audience and the odious Mr. Devereaux Winter, the last flickering flame of happiness within her sputtered out and died like a candle worn down to nothing.

* * *

"Am I to be your mistress?"

The cold question flung toward him by Lady Emilia took Dev by surprise. They had scarcely entered the small salon her mother had indicated they ought to occupy for the unprecedented occasion, the door just clicking shut at their backs, when she turned on him. And he had to admit, Lady Emilia King in a fury was a sight to behold.

Though her light-blue eyes flashed with anger, and though she gazed upon him as he imagined she might a lowly spider which had dared to scrabble across her floor, her stubborn, defiant fury intrigued him. Here was another surprise. He had not expected to want her as much as he did now, in this moment, desire for her clamoring through him.

He had always favored women who were golden-haired, buxom, and wide-hipped, lusty women who knew what they wanted. Lady Emilia had regal brunette locks, the pious air of a spinster, and the body of a waif. Her face was classically beautiful, as if she had been brought to life from one of the paintings he had paid a king's ransom to hang in his home next door. But the rest of her ought not to have inspired even a drop of lust in his veins.

Was it her disdain for him? Was it her bravado? Was it the thought of claiming and taming her, of making a duke's daughter his wife?

"Mr. Winter," she prodded, her voice every bit as cutting.

Somehow, the anger darkening her otherwise mellifluous tone only made his cock twitch. But now was not the time, and nor was it the place. Later, when he had what he wanted, he could indulge in seducing her. How delicious a challenge it would be to turn her ice into flame. He would not stop, he decided, until he had her, naked and begging in his bed.

"No," he told her curtly now. "You are not to be my mistress. Were I seeking a replacement to fulfill the role, you may be assured I would not settle upon a frigid, spoiled duke's daughter who possesses the figure of a chimney sweep and not the slightest inkling of true passion."

He did not miss the pallor of her already pale complexion. Nor did he miss the way she stiffened, her nostrils flaring, her sensual mouth tightening into a harsh, unforgiving line.

He had insulted her, insinuating she was not worthy of sharing his bed, that he already had a mistress, that she lacked femininity. In truth, he had parted ways with his last paramour some six months ago when he had settled upon the path which had eluded his father before him. The path of respectability.

The path he would use Lady Emilia King to travel. Whilst he was fucking the haughty disapproval out of her, of course.

"How dare you?" Lady Emilia demanded now, tiny grooves of fury bracketing her lush lips.

He wondered, for a brief, foolish moment, if she were somehow privy to his thoughts.

"If I did not dare, my lady, I would be dead," he told her after dismissing the ludicrous notion, warming to his cause.

"Better men than you are in the grave, Mr. Winter," she bit out. "A pity it was not you instead of them."

"I am sorry to disappoint you, my lady," he offered mockingly.

Christ, but she was an angry one. When he had settled upon his plan, he had chosen Lady Emilia as his future wife because of her impeccable reputation and familial ties. Her father was a duke, her uncle was an earl, and the King line was more noble than any aristocrat's. Even better, her father was ill, stricken with the sort of infirmity most families wished to keep secret.

The very sort of infirmity which would always make itself known, and often in a fashion most unwanted. The sort of infirmity which was easily exploited by the devils among men who sought to manipulate those weaker than them for their own selfish gain.

To the relief of his mortal soul, Dev had not been the man responsible for exploiting the Duke of Abingdon's mental frailty. But he did happen to be acquainted with the gentleman—a loose term, surely—who had. And buying up the vowels of the Duke of Abingdon had been easy.

Costly, but frightfully easy. When one possessed as much wealth as Dev, and as much determination, cost was a small matter indeed.

"I dare say you have not disappointed me at all, Mr. Winter," she said then, her tone still cool. Accusatory. "You are behaving precisely in the fashion I would expect of a lowborn rogue."

Her insult found its mark, burrowing deep.

He stepped closer to her, drawn as much by her beauty as

9

by the need to rattle her. "A lowborn rogue I may be, madam. But I am the lowborn rogue you will be calling husband soon."

She inhaled swiftly, as if he had struck her. "There would never come a day when I would so lower myself, Mr. Winter. If that is the reason for this absurd call of yours, I am sorry you have wasted your time."

He almost felt sympathy for her. But she was so arrogant, so cold, so much the epitome of every nobleman and woman who had looked down their noses at him and his family all his life, he knew instead a deep surge of satisfaction.

"I am afraid you haven't a choice, my lady," he told her.

Her nostrils flared. "There is always a choice, sirrah."

Dev cocked his head, studying Lady Emilia. Though she was slight, to her credit, she faced him with a bravado he would have believed her incapable of possessing. His opponents in business and in life ordinarily retreated within five minutes of any dialogue, recognizing futility when they saw it. But not her.

"Let me tell you what your choices are, my lady," he said then, "since you would insist upon having them. The Duke of Abingdon has recently lost a significant fortune at a gaming establishment owned by a friend of mine. I currently hold the notes to everything he possesses beyond the entail. All his wealth, every estate, including this home. Every bloody candlestick."

"Papa does not gamble," she denied coolly.

But her expression told a different tale.

"Undoubtedly, you are not aware of every one of His Grace's activities, Lady Emilia." He paused, gauging her reaction, infinitesimal though it was. "But I am in possession of a great many vowels which suggest he does indeed gamble, and further, he does it quite badly. He lost everything."

Her lips compressed, her eyes darkening with indignation. "My father is ill, Mr. Winter. He is suffering from a malady which causes him to occasionally act in an uncharacteristic manner. If he was making wagers, it was for that reason only."

To his shock, he felt something—a tiny tendril of pity—unfurling within him at last. "The reason does not matter. The results do. Fortunately for His Grace, I am willing to forgive the notes according to terms which are agreeable to me. Therefore, your choice is a simple one. Become my wife and save yourself and your darling papa and mama from utter penury, or refuse me, and pay the price for your pride. I am prepared for either occasion, madam."

Although, in truth, he would not rest until the woman before him was his. Something inside him had decreed it must be thus. And Devereaux Winter always got what he wanted. *Especially* when he had to fight for it.

"Why would you wish to marry me, Mr. Winter?" The look she gave him could have turned his soul to ice if he had possessed one.

He was reasonably certain he did not.

"I have something you want, and you have something I want, my lady. The exchange is clear and advantageous for all parties."

"Hardly advantageous to me," she snapped. "I would be forced to endure a lowborn brute as my husband in exchange for the forgiveness of my father's debts."

If she was attempting to irritate him, *by God*, she was succeeding. He longed to bring her tumbling down from her mountain of arrogance. To rattle her gilded cage and send her sprawling to the floor at his feet. "Just as I would be forced to endure an arrogant, joyless, coldhearted waif as my wife. But you see, madam, life is a series of compromises. To gain what we want, we must also accept that which we wholeheartedly do not wish for."

"If you harbor such disdain for me, why would you wish to wed me?" she asked.

"For the good of my family, my lady," he answered, truthfully and without a hint of malice. "I have already had contracts drawn up with your father's blessing, and he has signed them. I will forgive the debts I am owed, and in return, you will marry me and take my five sisters under your wing, helping them to acquire noblemen as husbands."

"No," she instantly denied, her expression growing pinched. "I cannot believe my father intends to…to *sell* me to you in such a fashion. Even on his worst day, he would not do such a thing."

Dev ground his molars. Why could the woman not simply accept her fate? "He has done what he must, and now it is your turn to do the same, Lady Emilia. I suggest you consider your options. I am a very wealthy man. I will provide you with a more than generous stipend. All I require is your assistance with my sisters."

He thought then of Pru, Eugie, Grace, Christabella, and Beatrix. He loved the five of them more than he would have ever imagined possible, and he would do anything—*anything* —for them.

He owned half of London. Along with the fortunes allotted each of them, all told, the Winter family likely owned half of all England.

But he had learned in excruciating fashion, not even boasting as much money and power as he possessed was enough to give him the one thing he needed most. Duty had been beaten into him by his bastard of a sire. Obligation was a Winter family privilege, second only to fear. But before all those came the incredibly elusive power of *respectability*.

The Wicked Winters had existed on the fringes of polite society for far too long. Dev was going to change that. And he needed the pale, unsmiling creature before him to assist him.

Strike that. She *would* assist him.

"I will not be sullying myself by aiding common hoydens," she snapped.

No one insulted his sisters, by God. He stepped forward, towering over her small figure with his tall, broad form. He thought he saw a flare of fear in her eyes, but it was gone in an instant as she faced him with defiance and an upturned chin.

"You will apologize," he demanded.

Her chin lifted an inch. "I will not express contrition for speaking the truth."

Devil take it, this interview was taking longer than he had imagined it would, and he was suddenly reminded he had a very important meeting to attend to. Instinctively, he pulled on the gold chain of his pocket watch, plucking it from his pocket. A quick consultation of the time confirmed he was going to be late.

Devereaux Winter was never late.

"I have another concern requiring my attention today, my lady," he said then. "For now, I shall grant you a respite. I urge you to make your decision wisely. Ponder it well. I am ruthless, but only when I need to be. Do not make me need to be."

With that warning, he bowed and took his leave.

CHAPTER 2

*E*milia frowned into the needlework in her lap. Thrice, she had stuck her thumb. Once, deep enough to harvest a rush of blood from the fleshy pad. She had narrowly avoided dribbling scarlet all over her partially formed bouquet of summer rosebuds.

On a sigh, she realized she had made yet another error. Her neck ached, for she had spent the night turning over in her bed, plagued by thoughts of the barbarian who had so rudely insisted she was to become his wife. When she had finally fallen asleep at dawn, too exhausted to stay awake another tormented moment more, she had been curled at an odd angle in her bed, leaving the muscle of her neck tense and cramped.

It had not improved this afternoon. More than likely it was because each time she thought of *him*, she tensed even more. Grumbling bitterly to herself, she removed the last dozen stitches she had made.

He was so tall. So large. Loutish, really, demanding an audience with her, speaking to her as if he were her equal, insisting she would be his wife.

She shuddered. The thought of becoming any man's wife was akin to a dagger in her heart. Her heart would forever belong to James. That a vexatious cur such as Mr. Winter could even have the audacity to believe she would ever wed him was laughable.

Rather, it would have been laughable, before Papa's illness.

Before Mama had told her, following Mr. Winter's departure the day before, just how dire their circumstances had become. Just how helpless they all were.

Mama's words still struck her. Everything Mr. Winter had said was true.

We are dependent upon Mr. Winter, Emilia. I am afraid you must wed him if we are to be saved.

As if conjured by her miserable thoughts, her mother appeared before her in the same salon where Mr. Winter had yesterday proclaimed she was to become his chattel.

Mama was wringing her hands, wearing a fretful expression. "Mr. Winter will be here soon, Emilia."

Her lip curled. "Tell him I am ailing."

"Emilia!" Mama's voice sounded as if she were on the verge of weeping, with a scandalized edge of chastisement. "I most certainly will not fib to Mr. Winter."

"Why not?" she asked. "You lied to suitors in the past."

"Mr. Winter is different," Mama insisted, her knuckles going white beneath the strain of her clasped fingers.

"Mr. Winter is unsuitable," she returned coldly. "But you require me to sell myself to him in exchange for what Papa lost."

"His Grace lost nearly everything we have," Mama snapped, her voice uncharacteristically stern. "Mr. Winter has done us a kindness in offering us the means to save ourselves."

"By using me as the sacrifice." Emilia stabbed her needle

into the rose once more, not taking heed of her actions. This time, the needle jammed even more deeply into her flesh.

She cried out.

"Emilia!"

In an uncharacteristic fit of rage, she flung the offending hoop, needle and all, from her lap. She watched it sail across the chamber before landing in a heap upon the Aubusson.

The *worn* Aubusson. Had she never noted it required replacing before now? Precisely how long had her father been draining his coffers? How long had he been ill? She leapt to her feet, determined to confront her mother. Not for the first time, questions clamored within her. Fears. Fury. Sadness.

She had already lost James.

And now she was losing her Papa too.

But she was also losing herself. She had imagined she would live her life a spinster. Mama and Papa had both known how deeply she had loved James. How impossible it was for her to even as much as think of another gentleman after his death. She would go to her grave mourning him.

"Emilia," her mother scolded again, her voice vibrating with tension, cracking through the air. "You have no choice. I cannot be clearer to you. The duke is ill, and he has been acting in an uncharacteristic fashion—"

"For how long?" she demanded, interrupting her mother.

"I beg your pardon," her mother said coldly, at last resembling the icy duchess who had presided over society for the last several decades as a stern arbiter of fashion and acceptability.

"How long has Papa been ill?" she asked, stalking toward her mother, the anger which had been building within her since her unexpected interview with Mr. Winter the day before finally bursting into vibrant, furious life. "It has not been a recent development, has it? He has been confusing things for some time now. Our chef has been replaced with an inferior cook. The carpet is in need of replacing. The roof is in need of repairs which have not been made in two years. I have not even had a new wardrobe for the last three seasons."

"You had no wish to wed, and it was not a necessary expenditure," Mama defended, but there was a telling tremor in her tone.

"You made it seem as if the idea were mine," Emilia recalled.

Her mother paled. "Emilia…"

Their butler Grimes appeared in the doorway, interrupting further conversation. "Mr. Winter, for Lady Emilia."

"Lady Emilia will be but a moment, Grimes," Mama hastened to reassure him. "Thank you."

Emilia waited for the domestic to bow and take his leave before turning her accusing stare upon her mother once more. "Papa has been squandering his funds for some time now, has he not? Pray, at least be honest with me, Mama, for the first time."

Her mother's eyes closed, her expression one of anguish. "I did not wish to burden you, Emilia. You suffered enough after losing your betrothed. I thought I could monitor His Grace's ailments well enough. There was no need to involve you…"

"I am involved now, Mama." Though part of her ached at her mother's pain, another part of her raged against becoming Mrs. Devereaux Winter, all to settle her father's debts when her mother had known he had not been himself for some time. When her mother could have done something —anything—to stop him from squandering and wagering everything they possessed.

The resentment inside her built like a white-hot tower, threatening to topple at any moment.

"Please believe me, Emilia, this is not what I wished." Mama reached out, gripping her arm, entreating.

But she tore her arm from her mother's grasp, the anguish inside her too out of control. "If this is not what you wish, then have Grimes tell Mr. Winter I am ill. End this madness before it begins."

Her mother's face crumpled before her, tears welling in her eyes. "I cannot, Emilia. You must understand. Please."

In that moment, facing her mother, the realizations she should have made well before now sitting heavily upon her shoulders, Emilia understood she had no choice. She would become Mrs. Devereaux Winter. And she would spend the rest of her life in torment.

* * *

Dev drove his phaeton with effortless ease, just as he had on so many occasions before. And like so many other times, there was a beautiful woman alongside him, it was the fashionable hour, and he was squiring her about with the intent of being seen.

What was different about this ride was his passenger. Lady Emilia King had spoken scarcely three words to him since he had arrived at her father's townhome. Her countenance could have chilled an icicle, and she was dressed in quite somber fashion. To look at her, one might suppose she was in mourning.

Hell, she probably *was* in mourning.

She did not appear any more amenable to his suit today than she had the day before. Once more, the agitated duchess had been hovering in the background, making certain her recalcitrant daughter observed her duty. At least they were alone now, beyond listening ears even if they were about to be paraded before half the watchful eyes of London.

Which was all part of his plan. He needed to wed the fractious chit. And soon.

To that end, he supposed he ought to make her speak.

"I trust you have been giving my proposal careful thought, Lady Emilia," he said at last, offering her another assessing sidelong glance as he drove.

She continued to stare straight ahead, as if the very sight of him were loathsome to her. "Your threat, do you mean to say, Mr. Winter? Surely it can be categorized in no other fashion."

"I am being remarkably fair to you, my lady," he bit out. "His Grace owes me a rather vast fortune, and I cannot help but to hope you are worth it."

At last, she looked at him. Her gloved hands were clenched tightly in her lap. She had the air of someone about to enter a battle. "Do you insult all the ladies you threaten, sirrah?"

"Are you this frigid to all your suitors, my lady?" he returned.

She was silent for several moments, and he wondered if she had resorted to her initial tactic of pretending as if he did not exist. His gaze cut to her, and she was looking ahead once more, her profile elegant. Her lips were full, he noted, when she was not flattening them into a thin line of disapproval. He wondered how they would feel beneath his. Cool and soft? Warm and supple? Would she respond?

Nay, he decided with a wry grimace. Lady Emilia would more than likely bite.

"I do not have suitors," she said.

"No suitors," he repeated, as though the revelation were a surprise. "Why not?"

In truth, he already knew the answer. Before Dev had

decided to pursue his plan with Lady Emilia, he had made certain to have his men make inquiries into her. The finer details of the lives of the aristocracy had never been a concern of his, and after he had hit upon the answer to his quest for respectability, he had been forced to make it a concern.

After all, though he required a wife of noble blood, he did not want one who would make him a cuckold. Nor did he wish to shackle himself to a woman with a tarnished reputation.

"I have no need for suitors," she said quietly. "I am content with my life as it is."

He maneuvered into Hyde Park along with a host of other carriages, noting she had not mentioned her former betrothed. By all accounts, her betrothal with Lord Edgeworth had been a love match. But Edgeworth had been thrown from his horse and killed before the nuptials had taken place.

To Dev, who had been born to the vast Winter wealth but none of the respect granted aristocrats, loyalty was important, even if it was loyalty to a dead man.

"What of Lord Edgeworth?" he asked, flicking her another glance to gauge her reaction.

She flinched. "You are not fit to speak his name."

Although he admired her devotion, it also nettled him. The notion of taking on a wife who not only detested him but still held steadfastly on to her love for another man seemed less palatable now that she sat alongside him.

"Have I wronged you, my lady?" he asked, trying a different approach.

"You have insulted me with your insistence upon a *mésalliance* between us." Her dulcet voice was still cold, steeped in rancor.

He sighed, for they had reached the carriage promenade,

and the crush here was even deeper. He wanted to court her, to give their marriage as much legitimacy as possible, the better to ease his sisters' glide into high society. If they were seen quarreling in the park, the scandalmongers would be secure in their convictions he had bought Lady Emilia as his wife.

"Perhaps you might at least try to smile." At his suggestion, he did the same, though it felt more as if he was baring his teeth like a feral wolf than attempting to woo her.

Lady Emilia brought out the worst in him. He had spent every minute in her presence thus far alternately wanting to kiss her and wanting to turn her over his knee. Much to his shame, both thoughts left him with an aching cock and no hope of relief any time soon.

She cast a furtive glance in his direction. "Why should I smile when I have been forced into going on a drive with the man who is also forcing his courtship upon me?"

He suppressed a growl, his grip upon the reins tightening. "I am not forcing you into anything, Lady Emilia. The choice is yours. I am merely providing you with sufficient encouragement."

"Threats," she said.

"Encouragement," he repeated through gritted teeth. "This could be far worse for you. Had the man who initially possessed your father's vowels had his way, you would be in utter penury. Instead, I am willing to allow your life to continue unaffected. If anything, your life will be better. As my wife, nothing will be beyond your reach."

"Nothing save respectability," came her acid response.

Of course, he ought not to have expected any less than her unrelenting hatred. Had he truly believed Lady Emilia King would be grateful to him for the clemency he had granted her family?

He sighed again, doing his damnedest to keep his false

smile in place. And to make it more smile than snarl. "Respectability is my sole aim, Lady Emilia. Hence this drive and the necessity of my courting you."

She was staring ahead once more, returning to her initial method of feigning he was not there. "I have no wish to be courted. The less time I spend in your odious presence, the better, Mr. Winter."

Well, that was rather biting. Whilst loyalty was a strong suit of hers, clearly kindness was not.

"I am afraid you will be forced to endure even more of my odious presence after we are wed, my lady," he reminded her.

She said nothing.

They traveled for a bit in stilted silence. Dev had to admit her persistence stung his pride. He well knew he was nothing like the lords of her acquaintance. But he also knew he was generally considered quite handsome, even without the lure of his massive fortune. The women of his past had all been pleased to know him.

That his future wife would so revile him did not sit well.

"Perhaps you might try," he urged her gently after a time.

She cocked her head toward him, once more rewarding him with the sight of her face rather than her stern profile. "What is it you would have me try, Mr. Winter?"

"Acquainting yourself with me," he elaborated. "The courtship will not last long, for I have not the time to waste. I have five sisters in need of direction, new wardrobes, and the social influence only a duke's daughter can bring them."

"I have already told you, I have no intention of aiding your sisters," she said lowly.

Before he could form a quip, she shocked him by smiling. It was the first time a pleasant expression had graced her countenance, and the transformation was breathtaking. Her lashes were long, he noted, her glittering eyes an unusual shade of blue, almost gray depending upon her mood. Her lips were even fuller when she was not frowning. Even more tempting.

And when she smiled, she was not just lovely. Lady Emilia King was bloody gorgeous.

If only the expression upon her face was for him instead of for the rapt audience surrounding them. With an irritated glance about him, he recognized the unprecedented amount of attention they were receiving. Apparently she had taken note as well.

He attempted to affect another smile of his own, but this too, he knew was more feral than friendly. He simply could not help it. Devereaux Winter had not been groomed to court and bow and act the part of lovelorn suitor. Any soft-ness he had once possessed had been beaten out of him by his father's fists.

"And I have already told you I can be ruthless when the situation warrants it," he reminded her grimly. "My patience for your hostility wanes, Lady Emilia. Do keep that in mind."

CHAPTER 3

*M*r. Winter did not just love his sisters. He
doted upon them.

Emilia made the astounding revelation the next day when
he and his sisters called upon her. She also made another
discovery during the visit: all six Winter siblings at once
were something akin to a whirlwind.

But that wasn't all she learned. His sisters' manners were
far more impeccable than she had imagined. Far better than
the surly Mr. Winter's manners. Fortunately, none of the
Winter girls resembled their brother in size, though the
eldest, Prudence, was something of a long Meg.

And she also noticed, much to her shame, that when Mr.
Winter smiled at his sisters, he was not just handsome. He
was charming, in a delightfully masculine, thoroughly rakish
fashion. When he smiled and he meant it, the depths of his
pleasure reached his dark eyes. His firm lips stretched. He
had two dimples, the left cutting a deeper groove in his cheek
than the right. And her body reacted in a strange fashion.

Her stomach tingled. Her every breath seemed heavier.
An unfamiliar frisson rolled down her spine whenever his

gaze tangled with hers, and her flesh erupted in tiny little bumps.

They were seated in the drawing room rather than the small salon where she ordinarily entertained callers, on account of the sheer number of them. Six Winters. All at once.

Mr. Winter seemed content to allow his sisters to conduct the dialogue this visit, and Emilia had to admit, she found it odd. Odd too to think of him as a man with a heart rather than the icy, unfeeling autocrat who had announced he owned her two days ago.

She shivered once more at her recollection as the most garrulous sister, Christabella, was in the midst of discussing her fondness for the color green. Green was not a color the flame-haired Winter ought to be wearing, but Emilia had no intention of offering her that advice.

Or any advice at all, for that matter.

She did not want the dreadful Mr. Winter to make further assumptions.

For even if his sisters were not the unapologetic hoydens she had imagined them to be, she still had no intention of taking all five of the Winter sisters in hand, even if her circumstances became more dire by the day. Just as she had no intention of wedding him. There had to be another way of saving them all from ruin.

Otherwise, she had no hope left. Otherwise, she would be left at the mercy of the forbidding, dark-haired scoundrel who had continually warned her of his ruthlessness. And yet, he hardly seemed ruthless today, in the presence of his sisters.

As Miss Prudence Winter interrupted her sister with talk of a foundling hospital, Emilia found her attention diverting once more to Mr. Winter. At nearly the same moment, he glanced in her direction as well. There was a tender smile clinging to his mouth, and for a wild moment, she could not seem to look away from that smile. For an equally wild moment, her heart thumped slowly, steadily, and a stinging surge of warmth pervaded her.

Their gazes clashed. A new rush swept over her.

His expression instantly changed. Hardening.

And something quite strange happened. She knew a pang of disappointment.

Absurd.

She flicked her gaze away, dismissing him from her sight and from her mind both. Instead, she settled her attention back upon Miss Prudence Winter, who was still discussing her charity work.

"Perhaps you would like to accompany us on one of our visits, Lady Emilia," the eldest Winter finished, sending her a tentative smile.

Dash it, she almost *liked* Mr. Winter's sisters. But she could ill afford to like them, or to be swayed by their convivial natures. Most certainly, she would not befriend them. They were sisters to the enemy.

She kept her own response carefully demure and vague. "What a generous offer, Miss Winter. Thank you."

The girl beamed, though Emilia could hardly think of her as a girl, for she looked to be of an age with herself, and she was already almost a spinster at seven-and-twenty.

"When shall we go, do you think?" Miss Winter prodded, beaming.

Oh dear. Apparently, Miss Prudence Winter was in need of some town bronze if she could not decipher when her invitation was being politely declined.

"She does not want to go with you," interrupted Miss Grace Winter. "Not everyone is as fond of smelly urchins as you are, Pru."

Emilia nearly swallowed her tongue. Here, at last, was

evidence the Winter sisters required the aid of a woman well-versed in the art of being a true lady. Refinement, elegance, comportment, and never speaking one's mind in mixed company were paramount.

"Miss Winter," she forced herself to say, addressing Grace, a sister she judged in age to be somewhere in between the youngest, a lovely blonde named Beatrix and Prudence, the eldest. "You must not chastise your sister in such fashion, and nor ought you to refer to anything...unpleasant."

"Such as smelly urchins, you mean?" Grace asked, sounding bored.

What a strange girl.

Emilia blinked, reassessing the half circle of Winters arranged before her. Her lady's maid was acting as her chaperone today in the absence of Mama, who had decided to pay some calls of her own after reminding Emilia of the necessity of today's visit with the Winters.

They are to be your family, Emilia. You must.

Emilia dispelled her mother's unwanted words from her thoughts, recalling Miss Grace Winter's query. She cleared her throat. "Yes, precisely that. Only, I must counsel you to avoid uttering such language in future."

Miss Grace Winter's brows raised. "How can one object to the truth? Infants are dreadful creatures. Have you ever seen one, my lady? If you have not, I must encourage you to avoid them if at all possible. Peevish and red-faced, all of them. Quite disagreeable."

"I think babes are beautiful," objected Miss Beatrix Winter then. The youngest of the family, she was also the most petite, and blindingly lovely.

"Oh dear," mumbled Miss Eugenia Winter. "Now Bea and Grace and Pru shall have one of their discussions. Those never end well."

Another middle child, Miss Eugenia possessed the same

dark hair as Mr. Winter, but, unlike the rest of her siblings, her eyes were hazel. She was also the quietest of the clan.

"Eugie and I try to keep our distance from all such discussions," Miss Christabella added then to Emilia, as an aside. "It is far safer."

Miss Eugenia gave an emphatic nod. "Grace has a history of pulling hair when in the grips of frustration."

The Winter in question turned her attention back to Emilia once more, but not before rolling her eyes heavenward in annoyance. "I have not pulled hair for years, Lady Emilia. I can assure you."

Emilia's eyes were wide as she struggled to form a polite response and found none. Perhaps she had been hasty in her judgment. She could see quite well now that while the Winter sisters had received training in proper manners—their forms of address, curtseys, and comportment had been largely impeccable up until now—after they began to feel comfortable, they forgot they were not the only ladies within the chamber.

"I am gratified to hear you no longer…pull hair," she told Miss Grace weakly.

Gads. Whoever attempted to launch all five of the Winter girls into society at the same time would require the constitution of a general.

Feeling his regard, she turned to find Mr. Winter staring at her in that contemplative way he had. He raised a brow. For a beat, she forgot they had an audience. Forgot about his squabbling sisters and the monumental task of seeing all five of them suitably married to titled husbands. Forgot about arguments, the color green, and all the reasons why she detested Mr. Devereaux Winter.

And in that moment, all she saw was a strikingly handsome man who wanted to see his sisters happy. All she saw was the smile he gave her: rueful. Hopeful. Wry. It was a crooked smile, and only one of his dimples appeared. He looked somehow younger. Softer. Gentler.

She wrested her gaze from him, turning her attention back to his sisters, reminding herself the Winter family was not her burden. Not her problem. What she needed to do more than anything was find another solution. Another way of repaying the tremendous debt her father owed the odious Mr. Winter.

* * *

With Mama still gone, Emilia sought out her father after the Winters had departed. The strange trace of warmth Mr. Winter had inspired in her had been reluctant to relinquish its grip on her. No matter how hard she tried, she could not seem to shake the recollection of that half smile from her mind.

Nor could she forget the indulgent manner with which he had presided over his wayward sisters, the unfettered tenderness and love in his gaze. The different side of him she had seen, one she had not previously believed existed.

It was troubling indeed. So troubling, Emilia grew even more determined to locate Papa and determine whether or not he had truly signed the contract Mr. Winter had spoken of. At last, she found her father, much to her surprise, not in his study where he ordinarily preferred to be, but instead in the library.

He was seated, his attention upon the book in his lap, but he stood with a warm smile at her entrance and even offered her an elegant bow. She noted his white hair was mussed, as if he had been running his fingers through it, and her heart gave a pang at how different her father was now compared to how he had once been. He had always been an august man, impeccably groomed. But since his illness, he had changed.

"Papa," she greeted him, wondering which version of her father she would find today.

Sometimes, he was gentle, others angry. Sometimes, he forgot her name or confused her with her mother.

"Emilia," he said, casting a weary smile toward her. "I have been thinking of you. Is it time for dinner already?"

"Not yet, Papa," she told him softly.

"I have not missed it, then?" he asked.

Her smile turned sad. "No, Papa. You have not missed it. Mama or I will always find you to let you know when it is time, you know that."

"Ah, but you will not always be here, will you, my darling girl?" He glanced down at the book in his hands. "Was I reading Shakespeare? I cannot fathom why. I have always detested plays."

Yes, he had. She glanced at the volume he held, noting it was *The Family Shakespeare* by Bowdler. Strange how something as seemingly insignificant as her father's reading collection could incite such sadness within her, but it did.

However, she said nothing of the Shakespeare. Instead, she turned her mind toward the other troubling statement he had made. "What do you mean I shall not always be here, Papa? Of course I will."

Her father snapped the book closed, his light eyes searching hers. "You are betrothed to Viscount Edgeworth, now. I signed the contracts myself. I hardly believe your husband will wish for you to remain here, looking after your thin-witted father."

His words sent a rush of anguish stabbing through her. It was not just the mentioning of James that upset her, but the reminder that not only had her life not gone according to plan, but neither had Papa's.

"I am no longer betrothed to Edgeworth, Papa," she reminded him, hating the tremor in her voice still. "The contracts you signed...do you recall when you signed them?"

A frown came over Papa's handsome, time-worn features. "Why of course I do, my dear. It was yesterday. Or perhaps it was the day before last. Edgeworth was understanding about it all. Quite a gentleman. Do not believe all the gossip you hear, I always say."

"Papa," she said gently, for even though his mind was not what it had been, in his more lucid moments, the reminder of his confusion tended to overset him. "I believe you are speaking of Mr. Winter, not Lord Edgeworth."

"I said Mr. Winter, my dear." Her father's frown deepened, and for a moment, he resembled the imposing duke he had always been. "You must pay more attention, Emilia."

"Forgive me." She paused, choosing her words with care. "The contract, Papa. Are you certain you signed it?"

"Of course I am certain, my dear." His tone was mild, as if they discussed something of no greater import than the weather rather than her future. "Is it time for dinner already?"

"No, Papa," she said gently, struggling to understand him, to filter through his words for the truth. His mind was a confused jumble of the past and the present, repeating and stumbling, and it was almost impossible to tell one from the other. "Do you recall the wagers you made, the vowels you wrote?"

He held up the book still in his hands. "I was reading, Margaret. I haven't made any wagers a'tall today. I have already promised you I shall stay far away from the devil's dice from this moment forward. It was only a weakness. I was so certain I would regain what I lost."

More sadness hit her, and Emilia had to bite her lip to keep the tears at bay. Her father had called her by her mother's name. It seemed now with each day, the man he had once been disappeared a little more. One day, there would be nothing left.

"How much did you wager, Papa?" she asked.

"Everything, I am afraid," he said, his expression turning stricken. "Emilia, I am sorry. Will you forgive me?"

"Of course I will," she told him, her heart breaking. She would forgive him anything, for he was her father and she loved him.

Even if he had sold her to the devil.

But one thing was apparent: if anyone was to save her now, it would have to be Emilia herself.

CHAPTER 4

*T*he hour was late when Dev returned to his Grosvenor Square townhome after spending the day with his righthand man Merrick Hart. A former factory worker who was like a brother to him, Hart was Dev's eyes and ears within the vast array of Winter factories and tenements. He was keen and sharp, with an eye for improvement and an understanding of the workers which Dev relied upon.

Ordinarily, Dev enjoyed his work, for he was no lord to the manor born, but this evening, weariness weighed heavily upon him as he entered Dudley House and handed off his hat and coat. A fire in one of his largest warehouses had destroyed a costly amount of textiles early that morning, and he had spent the bulk of the day planning a means of moving the undamaged portion of his goods and restoring the warehouse to a usable state.

Unfortunately, the structural inefficiency of the building in the wake of the fire suggested he would need to raze the warehouse and build a new one. Disappointing, though somehow symbolic. Dev was a master at razing and rebuilding in life. It was what he had begun a handful of years before, following his father's death. It was what he was continuing to do now.

"Your visitor is awaiting you in the blue salon, Mr. Winter," his butler said then, interrupting his turbulent musings.

The news gave Dev pause. "Visitor? I am expecting no one this evening, Nash."

Nash gazed at him, apparently unmoved by the revelation.

He sighed, rubbing a hand along his jaw. "The blue salon, you say?"

The butler inclined his head. "Indeed. She has been here for some time now, Mr. Winter. I sent her a tea tray."

She? Hell and damnation.

"Very good, Nash," he murmured distractedly, wondering who the devil his lady guest could possibly be. "Thank you."

He stormed down the hall to the salon in question. Surely it would not be Lady Merton. Would it? His affair with Alice had been lengthy and foolish, and though several months had passed since he had ended their liaison, she had yet to accept that he would not be returning to her bed. She still sent him perfumed letters, so frequently he had taken to simply throwing them in the fire rather than bothering to read them.

But as he entered the blue salon and found himself staring at the back of a diminutive form, he knew instantly he was wrong. Alice was taller than his mystery guest, and her curves much more pronounced. Her skirts were perpetually dampened. And if he knew Alice, she would not be halfway across the chamber, pacing agitatedly and wringing her hands. Rather, she would have been waiting for him with her hem raised and her thighs open in invitation.

All thoughts of Lady Merton were effectively banished

when his unexpected guest turned to face him, removing her hat and the veil which had been obscuring her face.

Lady Emilia King stared back at him.

Their gazes clashed, and heat settled over him, a languorous lick down his spine. "My lady. What are you doing here?"

His shock at finding her awaiting him in his salon gave way to a sudden rush of anticipation. And lust. He would not deny it. He wanted this woman.

She licked her lips, looking apprehensive. "I wished an audience with you, Mr. Winter."

He allowed his gaze to travel over her, assessing. She wore a simple gown, and she was buttoned to the neck. Her hair was dressed in an uncomplicated fashion as well. Nothing about her suggested she had taken care with her *toilette* prior to sneaking away to meet him. Nothing about her was sensual. She looked, in fact, innocent.

The urge to let down her hair, to unbutton her, to kiss her lush lips, to take that innocence and make it his own, struck. Need roared through him, along with a primal sense of acknowledgment. Lady Emilia King was his.

He stalked across the distance between them, not stopping until he was close enough to see her eyes were gray tonight by the glow of the flickering candles and the fire. Perhaps it was the hue of her gown. Perhaps it was a trick of the light.

Her scent struck him, and he had noted it before, but tonight it seemed somehow sharper, more dangerous. More delicious. *Lily of the valley.*

"You have already had an audience with on two previous occasions, Lady Emilia," he pointed out, his voice rough. He could not seem to stamp the desire from his tone. It was everywhere, cloying and unraveling and over-whelming.

35

She swallowed, making him take note once more of how elegant her throat was, how smooth her skin. "I wished for an audience that was more private in nature."

Private.

That lone word on her tongue, in her sweet voice, made his cock twitch.

Hell. Part of him was tempted to haul her into his arms, slam his mouth on hers, and kiss her until they were both wild with it. Until she would never again be able to look upon him with such cool disgust, as if he were her inferior in every way.

But she was not looking at him as if he were beneath her this evening.

She was looking at him in a different manner entirely. *Intrigued* was how he would describe it.

The other part of him, the part which generally tried to keep his inner devils under a tight rein, reminded him he required Lady Emilia to remain untainted by scandal. He also needed to avoid doing something stupid like kissing her in his blue salon at eleven o'clock in the evening. Because kissing her would inevitably lead to guiding her to one of the accommodating divans, unbuttoning her bodice, lifting her hem, running a hand up her inner thigh all the way to...

Damn.

He could not do that.

Would not do that.

He eyed her top button longingly. Perhaps just one...

He bit back a curse. "Private audiences are ill-advised and foolish, Lady Emilia," he reminded her as much as he reminded himself. "Allow me to escort you home before you do any further damage to your reputation."

"No." Her tone was firm, lacking the biting condescension with which she ordinarily addressed him.

Bold of her, first to steal away from her home—even if it

was only next door—and await him here, uninvited, then to gainsay him.

"My lady," he began, intent upon delivering the sort of sermon he would give to one of his own wayward sisters.

"Mr. Winter," she interjected. "Allow me to argue no more damage to my reputation can occur than being forced to marry a scandalous merchant and sponsoring his garrulous sisters in their searches for husbands."

Perhaps he had been wrong to think something had shifted between them during his visit yesterday with Pru, Eugie, Christabella, Grace, and Bea. He had caught her watching him several times, and he had sworn he had spied a glint of understanding in her blue-gray eyes before she had looked away.

"Whilst I am pleased you are no longer discounting my sisters as *common hoydens*, I am not a scandalous merchant," he felt compelled to defend. "I am a businessman."

"You are not my equal in the eyes of society," she argued, her countenance remaining unreadable.

"What am I in *your* eyes, Lady Emilia?" he could not help but to query.

"A man who loves his sisters." Her voice was soft. "I could see that yesterday during your call."

Yes, he did love his sisters. More than he loved himself. They were not just his duty. They were his blood, and he would shed every last drop of his in exchange for their happiness and futures.

He inclined his head. "I do. But forgive me, my lady, if I cannot help but to feel certain, given our previous interactions, you also see me as the baseborn scoundrel who is forcing you into marriage."

She looked away, compressing her lips, giving him her profile. But she did not make a move to retreat. "Are you not forcing me? You must know I have no wish to marry you."

"If you do not want to marry me, you have a strange way of showing it." He kept his voice hard, for he knew Lady Emilia King was a worthy opponent. "There is no more certain way of finding yourself married to me than being here this late in the evening, unchaperoned. If anyone discovers your indiscretion, you will be ruined."

She turned back to him, defiance flashing in her eyes, her chin tipping upward. "No one will be the wiser. I took great care to hide myself from all your servants. My mother has yet to return home from a supper with her friends, and my father does not even know who I am half the time."

Her voice broke as she made the last bitter revelation, and understanding hit him, along with something unfamiliar: compassion. It was an odd reaction, for he had learned all too well the art of mercilessness from his father. In his world, there was no room for emotions. There was profit and losses, numbers on a page. There was seizing whatever would benefit him, regardless of the means.

Rather like Lady Emilia.

Strange he should feel the tiny, undeniable prick of guilt now.

Small. No larger than a lady's needle. But there, nonetheless.

He cleared his throat, rejecting the unexpected weakness she wrought in him. "If you are seeking sympathy, my lady, you will not find it here. I am not responsible for the duke's ailing mind, and nor am I the man who accepted his wagers. I am merely the man who paid the highest price for them."

"For me, you mean," she said, and once again, those full lips of hers were compressed in disapproval. In anger.

And once again, he was tempted to kiss her. What was it about her cool haughtiness that made him want to debauch her? To mold her lips with his, to bury his tongue in her mouth, to make her beg?

"I did not buy you," he denied thickly. "I bought power. The power to get what I want. And what I want is a titled wife with an impeccable reputation."

"Are you so certain of that, my lord?" She paused, considering him, her gaze plumbing the depths of his. "It seems to me that what you truly want is guidance for your sisters. A helping hand to deliver them through treacherous waters. I can do that without becoming your wife."

The emotions swirling inside him went cold. He laughed without mirth. "Lady Emilia, surely you cannot believe I will forgive a veritable fortune in properties and wealth for you to play the friend to my sisters. If so, you are more naïve than I believed."

Her shoulders stiffened, and the color drained from her cheeks, but she still held her ground, standing firm. "What is worth the price of my father's debts? My virtue? If that is what you are desirous of, I will give you that. I will give you anything you wish. But I will not be your wife."

Rage seared him with sudden viciousness. She thought to offer him her virtue? What the hell did she think he was? What did she think *she* was, for that matter? The devil in him wanted to find out.

"What is worth the price?" he asked, repeating her question slowly.

Inside him, the anger continued to build. Anger at himself for leading her into such recklessness, anger at her for believing him nothing better than a depraved despoiler of innocents. He had never been more furious in his life except for the day his father had dared to whip Pru. But that had been a different sort of rage entirely. It had been a defensive rage, one of protective fists. This rage...it was dangerous, and he knew it.

But innocent, icy Lady Emilia King did not.

"Tell me," she said. "Name your price, Mr. Winter, and it shall be yours. I will give you whatever you want."

For the first time, he allowed himself to touch her. Just his fingertips upon her chin. Three of them. Without his gloves, he could feel her skin for the first time, smooth and bloody tempting, and warm, so warm. The opposite of her cold eyes and colder mien.

"Whatever I want." He stroked her chin with the pad of his thumb, knowing it was rough, not a gentleman's touch. Not giving a damn.

"Anything," she whispered.

"I want you on your knees," he said. "Do it. Now."

Her lips parted in an invitation she did not realize. "Why?"

"Because I wish it," he bit out. "On your knees, Lady Emilia, and do not question me again."

Her even, white teeth bit into the fullness of her lower lip. He almost groaned. This was not meant to be seductive. He had no intention of making demands of her. But somehow, he was as hard as coal, his cock straining against the fall of his breeches, and he wanted nothing more than to nip that lip himself before soothing the sting with his tongue.

She lowered her head and sank to her knees before him.

Fuck.

He was undoing himself with the lesson he was attempting to teach her in humility. All he could think about was sinking his aching prick between her pink, pouty, aristocratic lips. He had never wanted another woman to take him into her mouth more. Had Lady Emilia possessed an ounce of feminine cunning, she would have recognized the sheer lust threatening to overcome him, and she would have pressed her advantage.

But Lady Emilia King was a lady and a virgin, and he was merely attempting to make a point. He could not forget that, and the reminder that she was only offering herself to him as a means of escaping their nuptials chilled his ardor considerably.

"Tell me you will be my wife," he demanded.

She blinked up at him. "Did you hear nothing of what I have said, Mr. Winter?"

"I heard it," he growled at her, "and I did not bloody well like it. I want you as my wife and nothing else. If you are willing to humble yourself before me, then you should also be capable of managing the ignominy of marrying me in exchange for saving your family from penury."

Devil take the woman. Why did she have to torment him?

* * *

Emilia was on her knees before Mr. Winter, staring up the tall, muscled expanse of his impressive form. The carpet of the salon was thick beneath her knees, even through the fabric of her gown and chemise. And though the early autumn night was cool, she was hot. Her entire body felt as if it had been touched with flame. Her mouth was dry. Her heart was pounding. And all through her, the strangest sensation slid.

She felt as if she were a knot, being drawn taut. She was not meant to be enjoying this standoff with the unconscionable man towering over her. She was not meant to be tempted to touch him. And the ache between her legs in a forbidden place...it was altogether unexpected and unwanted.

Shocking.

Scandalous.

Shameful.

"I do not want to be your wife," she forced herself to say. "My heart belongs to another."

"A dead man," he said.

The coldness in his voice—or mayhap the truth of his statement—made her flinch. "Love does not die, Mr. Winter. If you think it does, then you are a more pitiable man than I initially suspected."

It was the wrong thing to say, and she knew it the moment Mr. Winter's expression tightened and his eyes, already so dark, turned obsidian. His jaw was rigid, his lip curled in a sneer that should have made him look relentless as he had warned her he was.

Somehow, it only made him more handsome.

But, like so many other things she was not meant to be feeling and thinking, this observation was wrong. Dreadfully, horridly wrong.

"What did you think you were going to do for me, on your knees, Lady Emilia?" he taunted, his expression grim.

Her face flamed, for she did not know. She had expected him to ask something of her. Something base and carnal. She had precious little experience in such matters, for James had been a true gentleman.

"Whatever you wished me to do, as long as you would set me free," she admitted on a rush.

But what she did not say was that part of her was curious. Part of her was drawn to this massive beast of a man. She did not know what was wrong with her. Ever since she had seen him doting upon his sisters the day before, hating him had become more difficult. When he had touched her, she had felt *something*. Something strange and raw, blossoming to life within her.

"What I wish is for you to be my wife, my lady," he told her then in his deep, booming voice.

Never before had she been tempted to touch a gentle-

42

man's legs. But Mr. Winter's were on display before her, encased in his tight breeches, so strong and thick. She did not touch him. Could not.

How shocking.

How wrong.

What ailed her? Perhaps she was as mad as Papa. That was the only explanation for the confusing mix of emotions roiling through her in this moment.

"I will not marry you," she forced herself to say. "Exact any other price, Mr. Winter, and it is yours."

His large hands caught her arms in a gentle grasp, hauling her to her feet. "Do you not understand, my lady? There is no other price. You as my wife. That is all I will accept."

She was standing now, his touch still branding her through the barriers of her chemise and gown. Their bodies were nearly flush. She tipped her head back. If she rose on her toes, and if he lowered his head, their lips would meet.

But she did not want to kiss him. Did she?

No.

Yes.

"Please reconsider, Mr. Winter," she begged.

He leaned toward her, bringing with him all his heat, the anticipation of something...perhaps the kiss she should not want...

"There will be no reconsidering, Lady Emilia. You will become my wife, or I will call in your father's debts," he told her, his voice harsh. Stern.

The opposite of a kiss.

"And never again kneel before a man who has not earned the privilege," he added. "Myself included."

CHAPTER 5

*D*ev could not shake the memory of Lady Emilia King on her knees before him from his mind. Two days had passed since her unexpected evening visit to him, and he was seated in his study opposite Merrick Hart, reviewing plans for the rebuilding of his burnt warehouse.

Or at least, that was what he was meant to be doing.

Instead, he was being plagued by a hard prick and thoughts of his reluctant future bride. Devilishly distracting to attempt to review plans whilst sporting an erection. Concentration was proving futile.

"What do you think?" Hart asked, breaking Dev's troubled musings.

What did he think? He thought he was going mad. Lady Emilia King had been leading him about London as if he were a randy stallion attempting to mount a prized broodmare. He had been courting her far longer than necessary, and she still refused to agree to wed him. Out of mounting frustration, he had finally given her an ultimatum. She had one more day before she would be forced to give him an answer.

And it had damn well better be the answer he wanted to hear.

Which was, of course, *yes*.

He sighed, rubbing his jaw. "I am afraid my mind is resting upon other matters today, Hart. What do you recommend?"

Hart raised a brow. "What do I recommend regarding the warehouse, or regarding the other matters troubling you?"

Dev ground his teeth. He had been in desperate need of an intelligent, trustworthy aide-de-camp when he had plucked Hart from one of his factories. Over the years, they had grown close, striking up an unlikely friendship. He trusted Hart implicitly.

"Both," he said grimly. "I seem to require counseling today, my friend."

Merrick pointed to one of the drawings laid out on his desk. "I would raze the remainder of the warehouse and begin anew, using this design. What is the *other matter*, if I may ask?"

"You may." He sighed again. "Have you ever courted a lady, Hart?"

Hart's expression became shuttered. "I cannot say that I have. Why, sir?"

"I am attempting to court a lady who is…reluctant." He paused, almost grinning at how ill-suited the word *reluctant* was in describing Lady Emilia. "I am having difficulty knowing how to proceed. In business, I seize what I want. I either buy it, or I make something better. But I must admit I cannot decide how to persuade the lady in question she ought to accept my suit."

"Use your charm," Merrick directed.

Quite sensibly, too. Except for one small matter.

"I fear I have no charm, Hart." He grimaced as he made the confession, for it was embarrassing.

His previous conquests had been ladies in search of illicit pleasure, experienced women who wanted a bed partner. Women who were attracted to the thrill of fucking a man who was beneath their class. The Wickedest Winter of them all.

"Perhaps you might try to acquire some," Hart suggested then.

Dev scowled. "How the hell do you propose I do that? One cannot simply go and buy it."

Moreover, the notion of him attempting to charm Lady Emilia was ludicrous. What was he to do, follow her about like a lovesick swain?

"Imagine, for a moment, you are the lady in question," Hart counseled, his tone contemplative.

"How am I to imagine I am a female, Hart?" he snapped. "Do not be daft."

Hart shook his head. "That is not what I meant to suggest. Think of what she might like. What are her interests, her thoughts? Are you scowling at her and ordering her about, or are you taking the time to ask her questions about herself?"

Bloody hell. He supposed he *had* undertaken this venture much as he did everything: with the vigor of an invading army general.

"What sort of questions?" he grumbled.

Hart grinned. "For that, I am afraid you will need ask one of the Miss Winters. They would know best what a lady might like to speak about."

"Excellent idea, Hart." Indeed, why had he not thought of it himself?

He had five sisters. Surely one of them could aid him.

As if on cue, a knock on the study door revealed one of the sisters in question. Bea, the youngest and the sweetest of the Winter clan, appeared at the threshold. The only blonde

46

in their ranks, she was as lovely as the rest of his sisters, but she was also the most reckless and daring of the lot.

Much to his dismay.

"How fortuitous, Bea," he said anyway. "Do come in."

He and Hart stood and bowed to her in deference whilst she dipped into a prim curtsy. Dev took note of the manner in which Hart watched Bea, and he knew a moment of unease before he dismissed it. Merrick Hart was far too loyal to pant after the sister of his employer. Dev was certain of it.

But as he watched, Hart's gaze never strayed from Bea. Nor did Bea's stray from Hart.

His eyes narrowed. "That will be all, Hart. Thank you. You may go."

* * *

Emilia was running out of time and will.

Mr. Winter would arrive at any moment for his customary daily call. Mama had been pleading with her for three days straight.

Accept his suit, or we will all be ruined.

What will become of your father?

What will become of you?

What indeed, she wondered as she stared out the window overlooking the small, terraced garden. It was early autumn but the hedges were still verdant, the syringa and Sweet Williams in fading bloom. It was a view she had admired many times before. But now, she scarcely took note of the pink and lavender blossoms.

Mr. Winter had given her a stipulation, and he was to have his answer today. An answer she was not ready to give.

A subtle knock upon the door of the drawing room heralded his arrival.

"Yes, Grimes," she called to the butler without bothering to turn away from the gardens.

"Mr. Devereaux Winter, my lady," he announced.

"See him in, if you please," she directed listlessly.

She felt, in that moment, oddly detached. As if she were inhabiting another's skin. As if it were not her, dressed in a pale-pink gown, her hair artfully arranged, the garden before her bright and lovely even upon such a cloudy day.

As if she were not the woman who was about to become betrothed to Devereaux Winter.

"Mr. Winter," Grimes announced formally.

Still, she did not turn. "Thank you, Grimes. That will be all."

Her lady's maid was somewhere behind her, applying herself to some needlework in the name of acting as Emilia's chaperone. It hardly mattered now. Mama did not care if she ruined her reputation, and neither did Papa. All they did care about was their own salvation. Papa because he was confused. Mama because she was frightened.

She faulted them both, and yet she could not harbor a grudge. Her anger was gone today, replaced by apathy.

She felt Mr. Winter's presence before she turned to face him at last. The same rush of awareness trilled through her, along with a heaviness and a fiercely burning warmth. So foreign, so unwanted.

He offered her an elegant bow, and not even she could find fault with it. She curtseyed formally. They stared at each other, the enormity of what was to come seeming to fill the silence. His dark gaze was intent upon hers, traveling over her face, lingering for a beat longer than necessary upon her mouth.

The bourgeoning heat within her spread to her cheeks. "Mr. Winter," she greeted him.

"Lady Emilia," he intoned, startling her with a smile.

A true smile, the sort he had bestowed upon his sisters with such ease. The sort that put his dimples on display and stole her breath.

"The flowers were quite beautiful," she told him, finding her tongue once more. "Thank you."

He had sent her lily of the valley, the tiny white flowers laden with a sweet perfume that matched the scent she wore. The gesture had been surprising. Almost unwelcome. She had wondered if he had noted her scent, or if the choice of flower had been inadvertent.

"You favor lily of the valley," he said, a statement rather than a question.

The choice of flower had been intentional, then, and must have been quite dear. The dainty blooms were delicate and past flowering season.

"I do," she agreed, flicking a glance toward her lady's maid. "Redmayne, would you please fetch me my needlework? I fear I left it in my chamber this morning."

Redmayne's eyes widened almost imperceptibly at her request, but she said nothing, dutifully taking her leave from the chamber. When she was gone, the door left slightly ajar, Emilia turned her gaze back to Mr. Winter.

His smile had faded. So too, his dimples. The startling charm of his initial appearance had been replaced by his customary surliness. He had not approved of her obvious dismissal of her maid.

"That was most unwise, my lady," he chastised. "Propriety—"

"Propriety can go to the devil," she interrupted him. "I wished to speak to you without an audience."

His lips quirked before settling back into a forbidding

line. "The last time you desired an audience with me, you appeared in the midst of the night, like a wraith. I suppose I must be thankful you have not resorted to traipsing about in the darkness once more."

A shiver went through her at the recollection of the night she had gone to him. The night he had demanded she kneel before him. She banished the reminder, sending with it all the unwanted feelings he had elicited within her.

"I thought you were a fair man then," she said coolly. "A gentleman. I learned my lesson."

His eyes continued to simmer into hers. "I never claimed to be a gentleman, my lady. I am myself, unapologetically."

Why did the wretched man have to be so handsome? She had believed herself incapable of feeling anything for a man after James. But Devereaux Winter had proven her wrong. To her great shame, anger was not the sole emotion she felt for him. There was, beneath it all, an underlying attraction she could not seem to deny.

"You are a scoundrel," she snapped, irritated with herself as much as with him.

How dare this unfeeling brute force her into matrimony? Yes, she must cling to her indignation. Else, what did she have left? Certainly not her pride, nor her freedom.

"Your scoundrel," he said, flashing her a feral grin. The divots in his cheeks reappeared.

She ran her tongue over her lips. "Perhaps. I have decided I will wed you on one condition, Mr. Winter."

"A condition," he repeated. "You are bold, Lady Emilia, for a woman in your position."

"And pray, sirrah, what position is that?" she dared to ask.

His lips twitched, as if he were struggling to keep his mirth at bay. "A woman with no option save one. Given the choice between penury and myself, I daresay, I know which one I would choose, were I in your slippers, my lady."

He was right, blast him, but she refused to give him a victory with her admission.

"I require a chaste marriage," she said instead, delivering her pronouncement suddenly, aware her lady's maid would return soon. For obvious reasons, this was a dialogue she preferred to conduct with him alone.

"No," he denied flatly.

"Mr. Winter," she pressed. "My heart belongs to another, and I have no wish to share the marital bed with you."

"Your heart has precious little to do with your body, sweet," he told her, his voice low and deep and dark.

Delicious.

No, she chided herself. *Dangerous.* That was what Devereaux Winter was. He was a barbarian of a man. Her enemy. A man who thought he could buy her and her virtue. He could purchase her future, but he could not have both. It was to be one or the other.

"That is my stipulation," she insisted.

She had not stopped loving James in his death. She would always, always remain true to him. That she must sully his memory at all by wedding Mr. Devereaux Winter was the greatest form of outrage. But she would do what she must to save her family.

Mr. Winter closed the distance between them in three angry strides. His legs were long, and when he was this near, he quite took her breath. He was so tall, his broad shoulders barely contained within his coat. And he was furious, there was no doubt about it. The slash of his jaw was tense, his lips set in a harsh line, his eyes dark.

When he was angry, he was somehow even more handsome. More compelling.

She could not look away.

"Lady Emilia," he said.

She stared, fighting the mad urge to touch him. "Yes?"

"I am going to kiss you now."

His words made a rush of molten heat slide through her, from head to toe. Her belly tightened. Her lips tingled. She looked at his mouth, knowing she ought to protest.

Instead, her hands settled upon his shoulders.

And he seemed to burn her straight through all the layers separating her skin from his.

* * *

To hell with charm.

Dev had tried it. He had sent flowers at Bea's suggestion. He had *smiled*. And now the vexing woman dared to tell him she would wed him but she demanded a chaste marriage.

Not.

Bloody.

Happening.

He gave her time to protest. But she did not, because like it or not, she felt the passion between them as surely as he did. She could deceive herself all she liked. Her heart may belong to a dead man, but her body was very much alive.

And he intended to prove it to her.

His hands reached for her waist. She was supple through her layers, soft. Her body curved perfectly into his hands, and as he drew her nearer, her breasts surged against him. They were full and lush, crushing into his chest like offerings. Her own hands were on his shoulders, resting tentatively, her head tipped back.

Her petal-pink lips were parted, her lashes low. She made no effort to disengage. She said not a word. Which was just as well anyway, because the time for speaking was done. He would tell her everything she needed to know with his lips and tongue.

On a growl of repressed desire, he slanted his mouth over hers. Gently at first, nothing more than the joining of their lips. She inhaled, as if he had shocked her. Her mouth was hot and smooth and full, and when she exhaled slowly, her breath melded with his. He deepened the kiss, his grip upon her waist tightening.

And then he could not resist sweeping his tongue inside her mouth, tasting her. Tea laced with the sweetness of sugar. A hint of citrus. Everything delicious. She made a sound of surrender, her fingers digging into his shoulders. Her tongue moved tentatively against his, but then with more assurance.

He hauled her even closer, until they were sealed, hip to lips. Her cool defiance had spurred his usual ardor, and now that he had her in his arms, her mouth responding to his, his cock was rigid and aching. He told himself she was an innocent. He told himself to show some restraint. To end the kiss before he caused a scandal.

But he could not.

Not yet.

One more kiss, he promised himself, and then another, and another. Until he was kissing down her throat, and it was every bit as silken beneath his lips as he had imagined it would be. He nibbled over the cord of her neck, finding her pulse pounding fast. And then he kissed his way to her ear, taking the lobe between his teeth and tugging.

She moaned.

There was no other way to describe the sound that emerged from her kiss-swollen lips. He grinned against her skin as he pressed another kiss to the hollow behind her ear. Dev could not resist licking her there. When she shivered and pressed herself against him more fully, he knew a swift rush of gratification.

Yes.

There was no doubt—she felt this. She wanted him too.

But his instincts reminded him they would be intruded upon all too soon. Footsteps sounded in the hallway in the moment before he whispered in her ear, "There will be no chaste marriage, Lady Emilia. I will have you in my bed, or I will not have you at all."

Satisfied he had made his point, he released her and stepped back just in time for her lady's maid's return. The woman's eyes flitted between Dev and Lady Emilia, assessing the situation. He knew how it must look.

But he did not give a damn. He had finally pierced Lady Emilia King's armor.

And it was just a matter of time until she was his.

Her stricken gaze told him she realized it too.

CHAPTER 6

*O*n the day she became Lady Emilia Winter, a torrent of rain lashed down from the sky, soaking all London. Emilia could not help but to feel it an ominous portent of what was to come. Summer was at an end, autumn upon them, and although Parliament's session had ended, many had still remained in town to witness Lady Emilia King wed the infamous Devereaux Winter.

Her new husband had spared no expense. Her wedding gown had cost several thousand pounds and had been made by the most exclusive *modiste* in London. Fashioned of silver silk satin overlaid with an elegant net, it was enhanced with pearls and abalone and trimmed with rich embroidering. She had worn diamonds in her hair, hanging from her ears, and circling her throat. The flowers adorning the church suggested Mr. Winter had emptied the contents of every hothouse in town. Vibrant roses and lush lilies had abounded.

To herself alone, she would admit she had been enamored of the glorious gown. She had adored the sparkling extravagance of the diamonds Mr. Winter had gifted upon her. The flowers had inspired sheer awe with their beauty.

For a moment, she had even reveled in the pomp.

But then, she had recalled who she was marrying, and why, and her heart had gone cold again. But it was difficult indeed to feel cold now, hours later, for she was luxuriating in a warm, sweetly scented bath in the chamber that was to be hers.

Scratch that.

In *her* chamber.

How strange it seemed to have everything about her life forever altered, in the span of one day. She had a husband now. She was a wife. And instead of living next door, she was the mistress of Dudley House, which was a good deal more sumptuously appointed than the London home she had known for the past seven-and-twenty years.

She had not requested a bath. Mr. Winter had, but it was warm and soothing. After an endless day of smiling for everyone and tamping down her inner sorrow that her wedding day had come and gone years after it should have and with a far different man as her husband than James, she had to admit, the bath was a welcome distraction.

Her wedding night loomed before her.

Her belly tightened at the reminder, and to her shame, remembrance washed over her, hot and seductive as the water. *His kiss.* He had only kissed her the once, on the day she had agreed to become his wife, until today. Every other day, he had been a perfect gentleman. Refined. Polite. Removed. Nary a hint of the man who had claimed her lips as if he owned them, who had shaken her to her very core.

Except for when he looked at her. Whenever their gazes clashed, she saw nothing but promise in his. And she hoped he saw nothing but denial in hers. But she was afraid he saw something else, something she did not dare even think about.

A door clicked open, disturbing the tranquility of the moment. She knew without a doubt it was not just any door. It was the dressing room door. On the other side of her dressing room lay *his* chamber.

Mr. Devereaux Winter's chamber.

He had come for her.

"What have you done with Redmayne?" she asked coolly without turning to face him.

She was uncomfortably aware of her nudity beneath the heated water. He would only need to walk a handful of paces before he would be afforded a full view of her naked body stretched out in the bath he had decreed she take.

But mayhap that had been his plan all along.

"No words of welcome, wife?" came his dark drawl, from somewhere over her right shoulder.

Wife.

When he said the word, she shivered, even though the water had been well-heated and remained quite warm, lapping against her flesh.

"You may call me *my lady,*" she informed him, determined not to allow herself to succumb to him.

"I will call you wife, as I see fit," he said. "Or Emilia. You are Mrs. Winter now, and you must accept your fate."

"I am Lady Emilia," she corrected, "just as I have always been, and as I shall remain. You cannot inflict your lowborn status upon me, Mr. Winter. I will always be a lady."

With that, she turned in the bath to face him at last.

A mistake.

He was dressed in nothing more than a banyan, as far as she could tell. And even in a state of dishabille, he was tremendous in size. Sculpted calves, massive feet, a wall of muscle, and he was tall, so very tall, towering over her. Glowering, really.

He remained near the door he had just passed through,

watching her with a hooded gaze, his brown eyes consuming her in the same voracious fashion they always did. And as always, something within her ached.

Ruthlessly, she forced it to abate.

"Are you enjoying your bath, Mrs. Winter?" he asked.

He was goading her. Toying with her the way a cat played with a mouse until eventually deciding to consume its prey. "What are you doing here, Mr. Winter?" she demanded instead of answering his query. "I sent Redmayne to search for some soap, seeing as how none was provided."

He held up an oblong disc, his lips curving into a smile that showed off his dimples. "Soap for my wife."

Was it the expression on his face, the powerful effect of those twin divots in his handsome cheeks, or the possessive manner in which he said *my wife* that made her stomach tighten and an unwanted ache blossom between her thighs? Whatever the source, she could and would ignore it.

"I requested soap from Redmayne," she said again.

And Redmayne was trusted. Redmayne had known her since she was in the schoolroom. Redmayne did not look at her with the heat of a hundred blazing suns the way Mr. Devereaux Winter did.

"I dismissed your lady's maid for the evening," he told her casually, striding forward, the soap still on triumphant display in his massive hands.

Of course, his hands were large, just like the rest of him. Her gaze shifted to them now, remembering the way they had felt upon her waist, gripping her. His fingers were long and thick. Not at all refined. Nothing about him was gentlemanly in the slightest. He was baseborn. Beneath her.

Delectable, said a voice within her, unbidden.

This, too, she ignored.

"You cannot dismiss my lady's maid, Mr. Winter," she snapped.

"You might call me husband," he suggested, still smiling.

But she was as stubborn as he was. "I demand my lady's maid's assistance in my bath, *Mr. Winter*."

"Dev."

She frowned at him, realizing she had failed to notice how near he had come to her—surely near enough to see her through her bath water now. She crossed her arms over her chest. "I beg your pardon?"

"Dev," he said again, pulling the chair Redmayne had set up by the tub even closer and settling himself upon it. "My Christian name is Devereaux, but everyone important to me calls me Dev. It shall be husband or Dev. No more *Mr. Winter*, if you please."

Everyone important to me.

Why did those words make her feel as if a spark had been ignited within her?

She scooted deeper into the tub, drawing her knees against herself, further protecting her from his view. "Give me the soap and leave me in peace, and I shall call you anything you like."

He smiled, and that smile did wicked things to her, much to her dismay. "That, I cannot promise. We are husband and wife now. It is my duty to tend to you."

"I absolve you of your duties." She waved a hand as if to dispel the ties binding them together.

Unfortunately, her hand was wet, and her wild gesture flung a stream of water across his chest, darkening the silk of his banyan. Good heavens, what would she do if he removed it?

He glanced down at himself, then back at her, a light in his eyes she did not dare question. "I take my duties seriously, wife, which is one thing you will learn about me quickly. Another is that I am a firm believer in reciprocity."

"Reciprocity?" She frowned at him, trying to understand

this complex man she had married, still so much a stranger to her.

"Yes." He dipped his fingers into the water of her bath. "If you splash me, I shall splash you."

He withdrew his fingers from the water and gave them a flick, sending a fine spray over her face. For a moment, she was so taken aback, she could do nothing but blink and sputter. And then she heard it.

His chuckle, deep and pleasant.

He was *laughing*, the wretch. Grinning at her, and he looked almost boyish. No longer harsh and forbidding, but somehow gentler. Here was the man who loved his sisters with unwavering devotion. He made her want to smile too, to laugh with him.

So she did.

For a bittersweet moment, they shared their levity, gazes tangled. He sobered first, his expression turning inscrutable as he reached for the towels stacked neatly alongside the tub. Tenderly, he dabbed the water from her face.

She held her breath, wondering if he would touch her. Wanting him to touch her. Their gazes held. But there was no graze of his skin against hers. Nothing but the towel, soft and absorbent and luxurious.

He finished his task, setting the towel aside.

"Thank you," she told him. "For the dress, the flowers, the diamonds, this bath."

Thus far, he had been surprisingly considerate. He was not, she had slowly begun to realize, the boorish merchant she had feared. He was far different from the man she had initially supposed him to be, and the knowledge left her feeling strangely off-kilter.

"You are my wife, Emilia. You do not need to thank me."

Something about the way he was looking at her now, the way he spoke her name, forced a new realization upon her.

She could grow to like this man.

* * *

If Dev did not proceed with caution, he was going to fall beneath his new wife's spell. The sight of her in the tub, her exquisite skin on display, her dark hair tumbling down her back, was almost enough to undo him. The sound of her laughter—husky and rich—had done something to him. His cock was hard, yes, but the emotions swirling inside him now were not mere lust.

They were something more.

Something far more potent, far more dangerous.

"Nevertheless," she insisted then, her voice tart. "It is only polite to express one's gratitude, Mr. Winter. You have been quite considerate for a man who forced me to marry him."

Ah, and there was the Lady Emilia he had come to know and expect. Acid-tongued and prickly. He grinned. "Dev, and you know as well as I that there was no force involved in our nuptials."

Her full lips flattened. "You hardly gave me an option."

"Of course you had options," he said mildly, beginning to roll back the sleeves of his banyan, one by one. "You chose me. Excellent decision, my dear."

Her eyes settled upon his movements, going wide. "What are you doing, Mr. Winter?"

He sighed at her determination to avoid calling him by his name. One of these days, he would take great pleasure in making her moan it, preferably while his tongue was inside her cunny. But he had time. And patience.

He would wait.

"I am assisting you with your bath," he told her. "This

soap is a new venture of mine, and I want to see what you think of it. So you see? Hardly the considerate husband you supposed me to be. I was thinking of my own selfish interests."

Everything he said was true—he had recently begun manufacturing the soap with a mind toward appealing to ladies such as Emilia. But he also wanted to touch his wife. Selfish interests indeed. He had been waiting weeks for her to be his. And now that she was, he was going to proceed slowly. With caution. However, that did not mean he would not attempt to seduce her every chance he got.

Beginning now.

"I am certain the soap is lovely, Mr. Winter." Her arms seemed to tighten over herself in the defensive shield she had created. "But as I already informed you, I have no need of your assistance. Redmayne shall do just fine. She is acquainted with my routine. Now please do send for her before the water grows cold."

He almost smiled at her resolve. "I do believe it is lovely, but I should prefer the opinion of my wife. We are attempting to rival Pears with our soap."

He was rather proud of his achievement in that regard. Soap was a new enterprise for him, having previously grown his father's fortune upon textiles and tenements. From the moment he had first bought a case of Pears soap for his sisters, he had been enamored with the notion of starting his own soap-making empire. He had not stopped until his men had settled upon a recipe which, to his mind, produced a superior product.

"Why should you care for my opinion?" she asked.

With her knees drawn up and her arms crossed, there was precious little of her visible to him aside from her delectable skin. He had never before been entranced by the mere sight of a woman's shoulders, but he was now. Emilia's were smooth and firm, punctuated by a collarbone he longed to kiss.

"Why should I not?" he countered, struggling to control the lust threatening to seize him.

The less he saw of her, the more he wanted her, and the more he wanted her, the more slowly he knew he must proceed. It would not do to frighten her on their first night as husband and wife. He was a large man, and she possessed a petite frame. She was an innocent and he...decidedly was not. Also, he wanted her more than he had ever wanted anything, the hunger so fierce, he could scarcely contain it. Not even the desire to build his businesses and amass more wealth could compare.

"You scarcely even know me," she pointed out.

Correctly.

He flashed her a half grin, ever hopeful. "A fact which I am doing my utmost to change, wife."

"What has soap got to do with it?" she wanted to know.

"Everything." Not true, not precisely, but the soap was a start. The bath was a start. Speaking to each other without rancor was bloody well a start. And they had to start somewhere, did they not? "I wish to know what you think of the scent."

Her lips tightened. She did not trust him, it was plain.

Fair enough. He did not trust himself in her presence.

She raised a brow. "What if I think it is horrid?"

His grin deepened, and the tension in his chest uncoiled, ever so slightly. Something inside him softened. "Then tell me it is horrid. I have no wish to lose a fortune on horrid-smelling soap, Emilia."

Her lips twitched as if she struggled to keep an answering smile at bay. "Very well. I shall smell your soap, Mr. Winter. But I must warn you, I will be completely honest, and if I do not like the scent, I will not use it."

"You are most fair, my lady." He extended the oval bar to her, holding it just beneath her nose. "It is meant to smell pleasant, all the sweetest notes of a summer garden. Your honest opinion, wife."

She inhaled deeply, and bastard that he was, he could not help but to note the way it brought the tops of her breasts nearer to the surface of the water and his heated gaze. "The scent is...lovely."

Her tone was reluctant, as if it pained her to give him praise. "You would use it?"

"I would," she conceded. "I will, in fact. Myself."

She plucked the soap from his hand. He could have tightened his grip, but he allowed her small theft. He wanted her to feel at ease with him. He wanted her to learn she could trust him. If she was not ready for him to touch her, he would grind his molars and bide his time.

"Emilia," he said then, his grin fading, for he was serious. "I know my means of persuading you into this marriage were strong—"

"Nefarious," she interrupted.

"Unfair," he tried.

"Dastardly," she said.

Well. He could not fault her. When he wanted something, he went after it, headlong, and without a thought for the casualties. He was the man his father had raised him to be: merciless, hard, sharper than a blade, and willing to cut anyone who stood in his way.

But something about Lady Emilia King—strike that—Lady Emilia *Winter* made him realize for the first time that his methods were not always sound. That perhaps he ought to have a thought for the casualties. That he needn't always be merciless or hard or sharp. That he ought not to have strong-armed her into their marriage in the manner he had, leveraging her father's illness and his debts against her.

If he had not, however, he knew someone else would have. And the results could have been far worse. Other men would have taken her as their mistress rather than as a wife. But he was not other men. He was himself, and he alone could answer for his actions.

"If I had not bought your father's vowels from the man who possessed them, things would have ended far worse for you than being my wife," he told her, for it was the truth.

Perhaps his only defense. And he wanted to defend himself to her. He needed to, because...because her opinion of him mattered. Because he wanted her to like him. He wanted her trust, her body, and *Good sweet God*, part of him even wanted her heart as well.

Her love.

What a strange notion.

Impossible, really. Improbable, surely. But tempting, all the same.

But then, she dismissed his troubled musings quite handily by pinning him with an icy, aristocratic glare. "Forgive me, Mr. Winter, if I have difficulty believing any fate could have been worse than this one."

Ardor effectively doused.

Gathering his tattered pride, he stood and offered her a polite bow. As polite as he could muster, given the circumstances. It was their first night as husband and wife, and she had dismissed him as if he were no better than a servant.

"Well, then. I will leave you to your bath and your contemplations of the other fates you may have suffered."

Without awaiting her response, he left her, stalking back to his own chamber. Even though everything within him called for him to stay. He would not push her. Would not press her. What he wanted more than anything was for her to come to him, begging. *Wanting.* He wanted her desire to match his. For now, he would settle for her as his wife. For the role she would take in assisting his sisters with finding suitable husbands.

He wondered if she had an inkling of the fate he had spared her from, but then he decided it mattered not. He was no angel. If he were, he would have bought her father's vowels and then forgiven them.

But he was a businessman. And he was the brother to five amazing, wild, wayward, lovely, intelligent sisters, and he had to fret over their futures. He was also the man who wanted his wife more than he wanted his next breath.

Damn it all.

He scrubbed a hand over his jaw as he tossed his banyan to the floor and strode toward his empty bed.

He did not need to worry about proceeding with caution.

He had already fallen beneath his wife's spell.

"Fuck," he muttered to himself, for it was the only word that suited upon such a revelation.

Distance was what he needed. Distance, time, and a well-formulated battle plan.

CHAPTER 7

"Good morning," Emilia greeted her sisters-in-law at the breakfast table.

This morning, like every other morning for the week since she had married Mr. Winter, all five Winters greeted her in turn.

And this morning, also like every other morning, her husband was, quite notably, absent.

The reason, she had been told, not by Mr. Winter himself but by one of his sisters, was that he preferred to rise at dawn, dine upon a light repast of toast and coffee, and then begin his day.

His day, she had also discovered, was lengthy. He was gone by the time she woke, and he did not return until after dinner. Sometimes, he did not return until long after she had gone to bed and fallen asleep. She would wake to the sounds of him shuffling about in his chamber, the familiar creak of a floorboard, the sigh of him settling into bed. And she would lie awake, staring at the ceiling, wondering if he would come to her.

He had not come to her.

Not since their wedding night and his unexpected foray into her chamber with his heated gaze and his bar of soap. He had not even spoken more than a handful of sentences to her. Instead, her days were filled with the tremendous undertaking of preparing his sisters to make excellent matches. New wardrobes had been commissioned. A dance master had been obtained. And Emilia had thrown herself into the Herculean task of hosting her first house party.

As the Winter sisters chatted in lively fashion around the table, she filled her plate from the sideboard before joining them. And she had to admit that today, for the first time, she felt almost at home.

Almost.

During her first week as a wife, she had learned a great deal about her sisters-in-law.

Pru was the eldest, the tallest, and she adored babies. The Foundling Hospital Emilia's husband funded was one of Pru's favorite places to visit. Next came Eugie, who was astonishingly lovely, but suspicious of everyone. Of all the Winter sisters, Eugie's reputation was the most tarnished, on account of a fortune hunter who had spread rumors about her after she had spurned his suit.

This, she had learned from Christabella, the most wayward of them all, who stood out with her lustrous red hair and her striking beauty and her penchant for speaking whatever came to her mind. After her, Grace, who was the most cynical of all the Winters, even more so than Eugie. She continually skewered Emilia with suspicious glares.

And finally, there was Bea, the baby of the Winter family. The only blonde amongst them, she was petite and almost ethereal in appearance, quick-witted, strong-minded, and kindhearted.

They were an intriguing mix, the Winters. Not as wicked as their reputations suggested, Emilia was discovering.

Indeed, the more time Emilia spent in their presence, the more she was convinced society derided the Winters because they had not been born of noble blood, and for no other reason.

True, they were...interesting. They were also far too forthcoming. Too openhearted. They possessed massive fortunes—each individually, as it turned out, for their father had allotted equal sums to his daughters in addition to the veritable king's ransom he had bequeathed to his son.

To her husband.

Her *husband*.

How strange the word sounded. How foreign. And yet, as the days passed, she found it easier to accept her fate. Perhaps it was because she saw so little of Mr. Winter. Or perhaps it was because he had seemed to accept her request for a chaste marriage. He had not even bothered to kiss her once again, and though she knew it ought to please her, the knowledge somehow nettled.

She could not forget James, she reminded herself as she took a bite of her eggs.

Must not forget him.

The brash merchant she had married could not possibly hold a candle to the elegant, refined, handsome gentleman her betrothed had been. James had been slight of build, his brown hair worn in tousled waves, his fingers long and thin, his countenance pale, as befitted a gentleman.

By stark contrast, her husband was bold, strong and wide and tall and massive. A contradiction: at times cold, at times hot, or soft and tender before cold and abrupt. His eyes were dark, and his hair was darker still. His soul? Very likely even more so.

Yes, she was relieved he had not attempted to force more of his kisses upon her. Delighted she had scarcely seen him in the last sennight.

Was she not?

"Is something wrong, Lady Emilia?" Pru asked, drawing her into the intricate web of Winter chatter at last.

The five of them were a cohesive group, and whilst they had been kind to her, they had been slow to welcome her as one of their own.

"Nothing is the matter at all," she said, flashing Pru a reassuring smile. "Why do you ask?"

"You were frowning into your eggs in rather ferocious fashion," Pru explained.

"You looked as if you wished to do them harm," Christabella added with a grin.

Oh dear. Had she?

Surely not on account of thinking about Mr. Winter.

"I harbor no ill will against my eggs, I assure you," she promised.

"I would wager it has something to do with Dev rather than the eggs, my lady," Grace observed shrewdly.

Emilia pinned Grace with a hard stare. "How much would you wager, Miss Winter?"

"Five hundred pounds," Grace said, unrepentant.

"You would lose it," she told her. "For I am not displeased with anything, and certainly not Mr. Winter."

"You must have wished for a honeymoon," Eugie said.

"Instead, you were charged with all of us," Bea added. "You must forgive him for saddling you with the insurmountable task of readying us for society. Dev thinks we must all marry earls and viscounts and dukes."

She was still adjusting to her new life, and to herself she could admit the prospect of finding suitable husbands for the boisterous group of women surrounding her seemed daunting indeed. To the Winter girls themselves, she would admit nothing.

"No task is insurmountable," she told Bea.

"He is forgetting that not all of us wish to wed," Eugie said, her countenance solemn. "Bea does not want to marry, and neither do I. No suitable gentleman would accept me as his bride anyway, after the damage that has been done to my reputation."

"We shall undo the damage," she vowed. She did not know how, but they would.

Together.

"I would only want a husband who would aid me in my work at the Foundling Hospital," Pru said.

"I want a rakehell as a husband," Christabella pronounced.

"Christabella," they all chastised at once.

"A rake would know how to kiss well," she defended.

"He would be too busy kissing his mistress to kiss you," said Grace, ever the killer of hope.

Emilia cleared her throat. "My dear sisters, I do believe our breakfast grows cold."

Insurmountable indeed.

A brief glance around the table proved all five of the sisters were making poor attempts at withholding their mirth. Watching them struggle to contain their grins proved infectious. She began to laugh.

And soon, the chamber was filled with the ringing, unrepentant peals of all their laughter.

* * *

Emilia hovered at the closed door to her husband's study.

After a morning spent working out the details of the house party she would be hosting in several weeks' time—short notice, and over Christmas, but necessary, she thought, to introduce the Winter sisters to suitors—she had learned

Mr. Winter was at home this afternoon, working within his study rather than traveling between his factories and doing whatever else it was he did in the course of a day when he was gone from Dudley House.

From the moment she had inadvertently made the discovery—through the housekeeper, Mrs. Rushton, rather than her own husband—she had been unable to dismiss the notion of speaking with him. She told herself she had a sound reason for wishing to conduct a dialogue with him. It was not because she wished to see him or because his lack of attention to her left her feeling a combination of bemused and perplexed.

No, indeed.

The soap.

That was the reason for the interview she was seeking with her husband. She had been using the bar he had given her on their wedding night for her baths, and she had become quite convinced it was missing a note. A floral note.

With a deep breath for fortification, she knocked upon his door.

"Enter," boomed his deep voice from somewhere within.

She felt that voice everywhere, like a caress. But before she could dwell upon that unsettling revelation, she swept through the door, closing it at her back. As she moved toward him, he rose from his chair, towering over his massive desk, diminishing everything else in the chamber.

"Emilia," he greeted softly.

Almost tenderly, she thought. A smile toyed with his lips. Was it pleased? Was it feigned? She did not know him well enough to decipher it with certainty.

She dipped into a curtsy, trying to ignore the manner in which he was looking upon her. "Mr. Winter."

"Dev," he said.

She wondered why her failure to call him by not even his

Christian name, but an abbreviated version of it, ought to disturb him so. Especially when he had not even deigned to spend more than a handful of minutes in her presence over the last sennight.

"Mr. Winter," she repeated pointedly. "Forgive me for the interruption. Shall I come back later?"

"Of course not." He moved toward her in long, lanky strides. "You could never be an interruption to me, wife."

Why did he insist upon calling her that? She did not like it at all. Part of her liked it too much. The emotions within her were a confused, jumbled hodgepodge as she watched him make his way to her.

Like everything else he did, he moved with a commanding elegance that took her breath. She tried not to admire his form as he neared her and failed miserably. He wore breeches that emphasized his muscled thighs and calves. Though he was dressed informally, wearing only a dark waistcoat, shirt, and cravat, he seemed more compelling than ever.

She forced herself to recall her reason for disturbing his solitude.

The soap.

"I cannot help but to feel something is missing," she told him.

His brows rose. "What is missing, and where is it missing from?"

Oh. She had rather bungled it, had she not? Probably because of the way he looked at her, with such raw, unfettered intensity. He left her confused. And overheated. And confused.

She ordered herself to abolish all such unwanted feelings and began again. "Your soap, Mr. Winter. It is missing something. The scent is not as full as it ought to be."

"My soap?" He gave her a knowing look, as if he were privy to her tumultuous thoughts.

"Yes." She frowned at him. "Your soap. I have been using it for my ablutions since you gave it to me, and I feel quite certain it could be better."

He considered her, his expression unreadable. "We have tested the recipe, the scents, endlessly. What do you find fault with?"

"The scent is not as full and alluring as it should be," she said, warming to her cause. "A hint of lavender is missing. And perhaps rose oil as well. Your soap ought to stand apart from its competition, rather than resembling it. Do you not think? I acquired some Pears soap and compared it to yours, and I find them far too similar."

His sensual lips drew into an admiring smile. "Quite enterprising of you, Mrs. Winter. I approve."

"*Lady Emilia*," she reminded him coolly. "You asked for my opinion. I merely wanted to give the matter due diligence. I would have relayed it sooner, but I have seen frightfully little of you."

Oh dear. She made it sound like a complaint. It was not a complaint, was it? She ought to be relieved he was not forcing his presence upon her.

His smile faded, and he took her hands in his, lifting them to his lips for a kiss. "Forgive me for my absences, my dear. I ought to have warned you I am a busy man, but in truth, I thought you may be grateful for the respite as you adjust to your new life."

Her cheeks went hot, and a tingle began low in her belly, trilling through her. The touch of his lips, warm on her fingers, seemed to burn. "Yes, of course. I am thankful you have honored my wish for a chaste union."

His gaze seared hers. "You are mistaken, Emilia."

He still held her hands in his tender grasp, and though she

knew she ought to tug them away, instead, she found herself gripping him back, her fingers tightening on his. "Mr. Winter?"

"Dev." His deep voice made her shiver.

The expression upon his face unnerved her. And the way he was looking at her—that dark gaze boring into her soul, it seemed—made her melt. *Melt.*

But she must remain strong. She must not forget this man had manipulated her into becoming his wife. That she had never intended to marry anyone. That he was beneath her in every way. Unsuitable. A merchant. Ruthless.

"Mr. Winter," she said.

He tugged her closer, bringing their bodies flush. Anticipation she could not shake built inside her. She was so near to him, the wall of his chest hard against her breasts, the firmness of his abdomen pressing into her softness, his warmth and his scent making an answering ache blossom inside her.

"Have you missed me, Mrs. Winter?" he asked lowly.

Of course she had not.

"I scarcely noticed you were gone." The moment she said the words, she knew they were an outright lie. She *had* noticed his absences. She *had* missed him.

And she liked being this near to him.

Her eyes dropped to his lips, and she swallowed, recalling how they had felt moving over hers, firm and knowing and masterful. Would he kiss her again? Did she want him to?

"Perhaps I have been remiss in my duties as your husband then," he said, "if you did not even notice my absences. I shall have to rectify that at once."

The wickedest part of her hoped he planned to rectify it with his mouth.

But then the stern, sensible part of her took over. "You need not make an effort on my account. I am perfectly happy with our marriage as it is. I have been getting to know your sisters, and we have made a great deal of progress with their wardrobes. Planning the house party has been keeping me quite occupied as well. And getting to know your domestics…"

She trailed off as she realized she was chattering like a ninny and Mr. Winter was looking at her in a fashion that made her lose her ability to think. He was looking at her, in fact, as if he wished to consume her.

"Emilia," he said, such tenderness in his voice.

"Yes?"

"You are protesting far too much." He smiled, and there were his dimples, in full, beautiful force. "Do you know what I think?"

"Yes," she said, flustered by the combination of his proximity and his almost affectionate regard. "That is to say…no."

"I think," he said slowly, "that you want me to kiss you."

He was right. She did. And she was drowning in mortification. In horror at her own inexplicable weakness for this man. He was all wrong for her. The opposite of James in every way.

She opened her mouth to tell him he was wrong. That a kiss from him was the last thing she wished for in this moment.

"Yes," she said instead. "I do."

CHAPTER 8

A yes from his wife's lips.

That was all it required for an unadulterated wall of need to slam straight into Dev.

She wanted him to kiss her. What the devil was he waiting for? He pulled her nearer still, their hands remaining linked, and he took her lips with his. The first meeting of their mouths since they had spoken their vows, this kiss threatened every carefully laid plan he had made to proceed slowly. To keep his distance. To remain aloof.

There was no *aloof* now. Not when she opened for him. Not when his tongue swept inside and hers moved against his. *Christ*, she tasted of strawberries, only sweeter. Not when she made a breathy sound of need. Not when her breasts crushed farther into his chest, until she strained against him, her hard nipples drilling into his flesh even through the layers of his shirt and waistcoat.

Not when her fingers tightened, when she rose on her tiptoes, kissing him harder. Something inside him—perhaps his good intentions, perhaps his control, more than likely his common sense—broke free. On a growl, he devoured her mouth. There was no other word for it, no other way to describe how desperately he wanted this woman, this kiss.

His wife.

Yes, she was his, *damn it all*, and there was no reason why he should deny himself any longer. She could fancy herself in love with her sainted former betrothed all she liked, but the truth was in her kiss. In the way her lips moved against his.

He may have married Lady Emilia King for all the wrong reasons, but the passion between them, here and now, was right. So very right. And he was going to avail himself of that rightness.

This moment.

He began moving backward, tugging her along with him, never stopping his kiss. When he worked, he paced, which meant he kept the path between his desk and the far window blessedly free of obstacles. There was no impediment now in getting her where he wanted her. They circumnavigated the massive mahogany piece of furniture, until they reached his chair.

And then he spun them about, all while drinking in the sweet elixir of her kiss. Her mouth was made for his, fitting perfectly, her lips lush and full, soft and warm and pliable. He had kissed dozens of feminine mouths in his life, but this one —hers—would forever ruin him for any other. This mouth was different from all the rest. This was Emilia's lips beneath his, Emilia's tongue touching his. This was his ice princess turning into a goddess of fire in his arms.

But kissing, as heady as it was, was no longer enough. He would have her say his name, *by God*. He would have her moan it. And he would bring her pleasure she had never known.

He tore his lips from hers, staring down at her, scarcely believing the flushed, glazed-eyed beauty with the kiss-swollen mouth was the same frigid and proper duke's daughter he had wed. Aside from the color on her cheeks, the dazed expression on her face, and the thoroughly loved state of her lips, she was as perfect as ever. Not even a tendril of hair had escaped her coiffure beyond the curls artfully arranged to frame her face.

"Sit," he told her.

She stared at him, her breathing as heavy as his. "Mr. Winter, we must not—"

"It is Dev," he interrupted. "And we must. *Sit.*"

She sat.

The ease with which she capitulated was proof of how deeply their kisses had affected her, he knew. But it was just as well, for he was lost, too. Swimming in the depths of a sea of need so endless, staying afloat was a moot point. From their first interview, he had wanted her, and with each interaction which followed, he only wanted her more.

He sank to his knees. Gaze riveted upon her, he lifted first her left hand, and then her right, to his lips for a reverent kiss. Then, at last, he relinquished his hold upon her. He missed the connection to her skin, to her.

There was only one way to remedy his loss.

But there was also one thing he needed to know before he proceeded. He only hoped she would give him the answer he wanted. His body was raging for that answer, for her...

"Tell me something," he said suddenly.

"What are you doing?" she whispered.

She did not move, however. Did not spring out of the chair or put distance between them. Instead, she watched him with her sky-blue eyes. Watched him with an innocent confusion he longed to despoil.

"When you kissed me, did you like it?" he asked.

Her lashes lowered. "I...Mr. Winter, this is inappropriate."

"You are my wife," he countered. "A more appropriate question was never asked between us. Do you enjoy kissing me? There is no right or wrong answer. There is only the truth."

"Yes." The admission sounded torn from her.

Thank God.

But there was one more thing he needed to know. "And when I kiss you, do you think of your former betrothed?"

He could not bear to say his lordship's name. Not now. Perhaps not ever. Jealousy boiled within him, along with resentment so potent it threatened to chase the desire away. He would not allow that.

"I cannot—"

"Yes," he interrupted again. "You can, Emilia."

A frown gathered between her brows. "I wish…"

"What do you wish?" He had to know.

"I wish you were the scoundrel I believed you to be," she admitted, a hitch in her voice. "That would make this far easier."

Before he could say another word, her hands were on him. Caressing his face almost tenderly. A foreign bolt of sensation tore through him then. Not mere desire, but something more. Something stronger.

"Nothing is ever easy, Emilia," he told her. The truth, bitter and real. Though he had amassed a fortune through his father and his own investments, his life had been a series of struggles and failure to be accepted. He knew who and what he was.

"No," she agreed sadly. "It is not, is it?"

"You still have not answered my question," he prodded. "Do you think of him when I am kissing you? When I am touching you?"

Her countenance changed, breaking before him. "No," she admitted, her voice almost hoarse. "I do not think of him."

Her confession felt like a victory. An arrow of heat went straight to his loins.

"Good," he told her, pressing a kiss to the palm of each of her hands. And then, he grasped her wrists gently in his hands, extricating himself from her hold. He placed her hands in her lap.

"What are you doing, Mr. Winter?" she demanded, her eyes going wide as he grasped the hems of her gown and chemise in both his hands and began to drag them slowly upward.

Her refusal to call him by his name irked him.

"What does it look like I am doing, *Mrs. Winter*?" he returned, lifting her hem past her calves. "I am raising your skirts, just as I ought to have done on our wedding night."

"It is the midst of the day." Her tone was scandalized.

And yet, she made no move to stop him.

He suppressed a grin at the knowledge. He would cease this mad game they played, of course, at the slightest hint on her part that she did not want to indulge in the mad fire roaring between them every bit as much as he did. Until then, he would continue to torture them both with a slow and steady seduction.

"You came to me," he pointed out, watching the progress of his efforts. Her hem had now lifted above her knees.

She kept them pressed together, as if guarding herself against the revelation of her greatest secret. And perhaps she was, in a way.

"To speak of soap." She was breathless now.

He reached the tops of her thighs. "You could have sent me a note."

"Is that what you would prefer, Mr. Winter?"

Blast the stubborn woman. He ground his molars. "I would like for you to call me Dev as I have asked."

"You are still very much a stranger to me," she said softly. "I would prefer to wait until we are better acquainted."

He was about to acquaint them. Quite intimately.

"We know each other well enough, Emilia." As he lifted her skirts to pool in a soft, expensive puddle about her waist, he caressed her thighs. His fingers found the ribbons keeping her stockings in place, but he did not yet move to untie them. Beneath the silk, her thighs were well-curved and strong. Creamy and pale where the sun never touched. Forbidden and delicious and his.

All his.

And he wanted to worship her. He kissed first one knee, then the other, his hands gently gliding over the legs he had revealed all the while. Just her outer thighs, soothing over the smoothness of her hips. Here, she smelled of soap. *His* soap, he realized. Womanly and flowery. A goddess in a garden.

Fuck.

All Emilia had to do was appear in his study, and he was gone. On his knees, a supplicant before her. She had him, and she did not even know it. *Thank Christ* she did not know it. For if she did…

"Mr. Winter," she said again. Not a protest really, but a sigh. She moved. Writhed. Her knees parted ever so slightly.

"Dev." He kissed her inner right thigh, her inner left. Stockings still kept his mouth from what he wanted most: the taste of her bare skin.

"Mr.—*oh*," she began, only to trail off when his hands worked their way down her legs once more.

He lost his patience. There was nothing more he wanted in that moment than to hear his Christian name upon her lips and watch her thighs open to him. He returned to the ribbons holding her stockings in place. A few deft plucks, and they were undone. He rolled her stockings down her legs.

He wanted nothing between them. No barriers. No silk. No lies, no pretending. He wanted only Emilia and Dev. Husband and wife. Real and true. Desire, raw and real. Her slippers came off with ease. Her stockings, too, were gone. And then he had nothing but bare legs, sweet curves, and temptation.

Even her feet were beautiful, *by God*. Delicate and dainty. Had he ever noticed something as trivial as a woman's foot before? He did not recall ever having done so. He took her right foot in his hand, pressing a kiss to the high arch, and feeling her shiver against him in response.

She liked it.

Excellent to know.

He kissed her ankle next. She gasped.

"What are you doing?" she asked again, but there was no censure in her voice this time. In its place was a blatant, desperate tone of want.

She hungered for him too. The knowledge was not just reassuring. It was humbling. Thrilling.

"Making amends for my absence," he said, as he kissed his way up her inner calf. "I would not wish for my bride to think me a poor husband, after all."

"Oh." She was more breathless than ever. "I could never... I do not..."

Speechless.

He smiled against her skin. He had rendered her speechless, and he had yet to even pleasure her in truth. "You are wrong," he murmured in between kisses up her calves. "You could, and you do." More kisses. "You will."

He could not wait to melt her ice.

"You ought not..."

Even her protests drifted away as he kissed her inner thigh. As her legs opened for him. He did not even need to guide her or to ask. A glance up her body revealed her lovely face: lips parted, eyes glazed and dark, more gray than blue. Her breath left her in small pants.

"What should I not do, Emilia?" he rasped, caressing her

hips. The heat of her was enough to scald him. The scent of her, musky and floral, singed his senses.

"Everything," she said. "Nothing. I do not know."

His gaze never leaving hers, he kissed her thigh again, flicking his tongue over her this time. "Shall I stop?"

Say no, he thought desperately. *Say no.*

But he would stop if she wished it.

He hoped like hell she didn't wish it.

"I…what are you doing?" she asked, breathless.

Of course. What a thoughtless scoundrel he was acting. She was an innocent, a different creature entirely from the experienced ladies he had known in his past. Perhaps she thought he meant to consummate their union here, upon his bloody chair.

"Bringing you pleasure, darling," he said softly, continuing to stroke her thighs in soothing, rhythmic motions, much as he would a spooked horse. "I am not a complete beast, though you may think the worst of me. I have no intention of bedding you here."

She swallowed. "Pleasure."

Ah, sweet Christ. The mere utterance of the word on her lips.

He suppressed a groan. "Pleasure, Emilia. Will you let me show you?"

Slowly, he told himself. *Recall your plan.*

"Yes," she whispered.

And there it was, the sweetest word ever to be issued in her dulcet voice, for the second time.

He did not hesitate. Still holding her gaze, he kissed his way higher, all the way up her inner thigh. When he reached her mound, he kissed her there as well. Just one press of his lips to her molten center. She jerked against him, the breath leaving her.

A mere kiss was not enough. Would never be enough. He

licked along her seam, lightly running his tongue over her, acquainting the both of them with the newness of it. She was sweet on his tongue, silken, and warm, so very warm. He parted her folds, unable to help himself. And still, his eyes never left hers as he pleasured her.

She was first to sever the contact, closing her eyes, almost as if the intensity was too much for her to withstand. But he had only just begun. He was not done with her yet. He would never be done with her.

His tongue found the sensitive bundle of flesh he knew would be most responsive. He flicked over the nub. She jerked against him, crying out. Dev was like a starving man who had been laid before a feast. From the moment he had decided he would wed Lady Emilia King, he had wanted her. Now, at long last, he was having her.

His base instincts took the reins, then. His hands slid beneath her bottom, cupping her, and he hauled her closer to him, angling her cunny into his face. She was delicious, and wet, so very wet. Even if her mind did not want him, her body had different ideas, and he knew it now.

Her hands settled in his hair, but instead of pushing him away, her fingers tunneled through, sifting the strands, her nails abrading his scalp. Her ardor spurred him on. He sucked her pearl, and she cried out again.

"Dev!"

Bloody hell. She had said his name at long last. If he had known what she required to call him by his Christian name before, he would have been on his knees long ago. Either way, he was determined to make her say it again. And again.

And again.

He sucked her pearl, rewarding her, and she bucked, writhing against him. He nipped her with his teeth, then alternated between licking, sucking, and biting until she was pumping her hips, gasping, desperate.

Until she needed him to give her the release only he could provide.

Dev was as lost in her as she was in him. The taste of her, the scent of her, the throaty cries she made, the sheer responsiveness of her body, moving and undulating against him, her hands holding him to her, all of her demanding more, taking more, needing more...

He fluttered his tongue over her channel, delving inside, not deep enough to break her maidenhead, just a gentle dip. She was so slick, and his cock ached in his breeches with the need to be buried home within her. But he could not. This was about Emilia. About Emilia's pleasure. About showing his wife she was not fashioned of ice, but rather of fire.

He worked his way lower still, running his tongue over a more forbidden place. She jerked against him, her hands tightening on his hair with almost painful persistence. This, too, she liked. Also most excellent to know.

But that was an exploration for another day.

He teased her once more with another slow flutter of his tongue, and then he licked a path to her pearl. This time, when he sucked, he knew she was close to spending. Her body was moving faster, and the tension emanating from her was almost palpable. She needed this release as much as he did. He sucked harder, then gently caught her between his teeth and tugged.

It was all she needed.

She came, crying out his name, her body convulsing with tiny paroxysms of pleasure. It was only through the utmost exertion of control that he did not. His cock was rigid and painful, his ballocks drawn tight. His breeches felt as if they were choking the life from him. But he would not spend until he was inside her. He was determined.

Dev ran his tongue over her in soothing strokes, bringing her back down from the maddening heights of desire, greedily lapping up the evidence of her spend. All he could taste, smell, and see, was Emilia. His glorious wife. Her equally glorious pleasure.

Tonight was the night to consummate their union. He felt certain of it.

Forcing himself to withdraw, he pressed a wet kiss to each of her inner thighs before rocking back on his heels. Their gazes clung, and for a moment, he was treated to the most erotic sight he had ever beheld: Emilia seated on his chair, flushed with desire, skirts lifted to her waist, thighs open, her dripping pink cunny on full display. It was all he could do to keep himself from burying his face between her legs again and making her spend once more.

But he had no wish to scare her away or to push her further than she was prepared to go. She was his wife, he reminded himself, and they had a lifetime to learn each other. To please each other. Moreover, she still considered herself in love with a dead man.

The reminder sufficiently cooled his ardor, enough so that he flipped the hems of her chemise and gown back into place. She was once more covered and demure before him. To gaze upon her, one would never guess she had just been ruthlessly pleasured. The only signs were the flush in her cheeks and the swell of her pupils.

"Would you have me come to you tonight, Emilia?" he asked, yet on his knees and certain, so certain, of her answer after what they had just shared.

But his question had the opposite of its intended effect.

Her countenance shuttered. The desire dismantled in an instant. She flew from his chair as if it had burned her, standing over him, looking stricken. "No. No, you must not. And I cannot. *We* cannot. This was wicked, and it cannot happen again!"

He rose, disliking her towering over him, and reached for

her. "Emilia, calm yourself. We are husband and wife. There is nothing wrong in what we just shared."

She shrugged away from his touch, and that was when he noticed a shimmer in her eyes, a teardrop on her cheek. "But I do not love you, Mr. Winter. My heart belongs to another. And I fear I...I must go."

With that, she dashed around him, fleeing from his study with such haste he feared she would trip over her hem. But she did not, and when the door slammed at her back, he flinched. Not as much because of the jarring dissonance of the sound as because of the similitude it held to her words.

I do not love you, Mr. Winter.

My heart belongs to another.

He gritted his teeth. To the bloody devil with that. The heart of Mrs. Devereaux Winter could only belong to one man, and that was *him*, damn it. He just needed to find a means of winning it. Surely he could find a way to secure victory against a ghost, could he not?

Curse it. And curse the Viscount Edgeworth. Dev was jealous of a dead man.

CHAPTER 9

Emilia devoted herself to distraction, studiously avoiding her husband. More shopping with her sisters-in-law, more planning for the country house party. More visits with her mother and father—since they were situated just next door, disappearing there was becoming a regular occurrence.

It had been precisely four days since she had last encountered her husband in his study. Since he had brought her to the shattering heights of pleasure. And since she had promptly toppled down into the valley of shame.

He had not come to her in her chamber. Nor had he been present at breakfast or dinner. Nary a word. Not a note. Simply silence. And absence.

Which was just as well, she reminded herself as she sat opposite Mama upon a chair in her mother's favored salon. They were taking tea. Another excellent form of diversion. Not that she required diversion. Or that she cared her husband had not bothered to touch or kiss her since her ill-fated trip into his territory.

No, indeed.

"How is Papa?" she asked her mother, taking a sip of her tea.

Her father's health was a constant source of worry for her. Though she visited frequently, she knew from experience that her father's moods and lucidity could shift quite easily. Though he had seemed in good spirits whenever she saw him, that did not necessarily mean he was doing well. He was changeable as the wind.

"His Grace is doing much better since Mr. Winter sent Mr. Rhodes to us a few days ago." Her mother settled her teacup back in its saucer. "You must thank him for us, my dear."

Emilia frowned. "I had no idea Mr. Winter had sent anyone. Who is this Mr. Rhodes?"

"He is a lovely young gentleman," Mama said. "His father is a vicar, and his mother was a baron's daughter. We are so fortunate to find a gentleman who is well accustomed to those suffering from the same ailment as Abingdon. Mr. Rhodes is patient and kind, and he rather reminds your father of a friend he had in his youth."

Her mother did not easily heap praise upon others. Emilia's suspicions were further raised. "What did Mr. Winter have to do with this Mr. Rhodes character, again?"

"Mr. Winter hired him to assist His Grace," Mama answered, smiling brightly. "I supposed you already knew. Mr. Winter had the notion that if your father had a companion, of sorts, someone to look after him, he may not so easily find himself in further...scrapes."

"Ah." Discomfited, she stared down into her tea, as if it would provide her with the answers she sought. "How thoughtful of Mr. Winter."

Unusually so, she thought.

But then she realized, not for the first time, how much of a stranger her husband remained to her. He had kissed her.

He had worshiped her body, brought her great pleasure. He had married her. And yet, she scarcely knew him, the man she had wed.

The man who concerned himself with her father's illness in a compassionate manner. The man who was perhaps not all he had seemed to be. The man who was, perhaps, far more.

"He is not the man I supposed him to be, Emilia," Mama said then, in an eerie echo of the bent of her own muddled thoughts.

Her gaze jerked from the tea back to her mother. "Is he not?"

"His reputation precedes him." Her mother's smile turned wistful. "But I have been persuaded to understand it is not always the rumors that make a gentleman. When he first approached us about your father's debts and his desire to marry you, I feared the worst. His actions, however, have proven otherwise. And you, dearest daughter, are you happy?"

Was she? She could not say she was. But neither could she say she was unhappy either. She lived in a grim state of the in-between. One foot in her old life, the other upon slippery ground in the new.

"I am well," she said at last, for this, in itself, was true.

She *was* well. Just confused.

"I know you loved Edgeworth and you had no wish to marry another," Mama said then, her voice comforting. "But you cannot live in the past, Emilia. Try to be happy with Mr. Winter. Promise me you shall."

Emilia lifted her teacup to her lips rather than responding.

She was far too old to make promises she was not sure she could keep.

* * *

Emilia returned from tea with her mother and immediately sought refuge in the calm stillness of her chamber. Though she had begun to think of Pru, Eugie, Christabella, Grace, and Bea as her own sisters, her heart was heavy today. Burdened by revelations and uncertainty. And what she wanted—what she needed—was some quiet to sift through her emotions.

What she did not expect, however, was the crate awaiting her upon her bed. Frowning, she crossed the chamber to inspect its contents. There was a note penned in bold, masculine scrawl laid upon the top. She picked it up, hastily scanning it.

Dearest Emilia,
You were right about the soap, of course.
Yours,
Dev

Beneath the note, the crate was laden with at least a dozen oblong discs of soap. She retrieved one, raised it to her nose, and took a delicate sniff in spite of herself. And also in spite of herself, she had to admit the scent of the soap was now perfect. It was rich and elegant, redolent with floral notes in a perfect blend.

She wondered then if he had delivered the soap himself or if he had ordered a servant to take on the task. Then she wondered, just as quickly, why it mattered. But she knew, as she held the note from him in one hand, the soap in the other.

The thought of Devereaux Winter inside her chamber did strange things to her.

It made her pulse quicken.

It made the flesh between her thighs come to life, throbbing with a new ache.

It made her wish she had been there to accept the delivery, if indeed he had been the one to make it.

Mr. Winter had altered the recipe of his soap at her suggestion. He had hired a companion for her father. He had not demanded she share the marriage bed with him as her mother had cautioned her prior to their nuptials was his right. He had kissed her as if she were precious to him. He had sank to his knees before her.

And he had given her the sort of pleasure she had never known was possible.

Her mother's words echoed in her mind as she stared, bemused, at the soap and the note, the twin symbols of how Mr. Devereaux Winter was far more complex than she had ever supposed.

You cannot live in the past, Emilia.

Did she dare to move forward? And did she dare trust the man she had married?

She did not know yet.

What she *did* know was that she needed to try the soap. A bath, if nothing else, would prove restorative. Besides, if Mr. Winter had changed the recipe of his soap at her suggestion, the least she could do was make use of his latest creation. It was not as if she was searching for a reason to seek him out. No, indeed. She was merely being polite.

Returning his gesture with one of her own.

That was it.

That was *all*.

Oh, who was she fooling? She wanted to see her husband again. Of course she did. How could she not? And mayhap to kiss him. Mayhap to see where this union of theirs could lead.

She placed the soap back in its crate, but she kept the note, folding it before crossing the chamber and tucking it between the pages of her journal. Some strange instinct inside her made her want to keep that note, its spare sentence, the bold slant of his scrawl. Something about it had rather touched her heart.

Much like the man who had written it.

* * *

For the first time in as long as he could recall, Dev returned to Dudley House early. It was late afternoon, and he ought to have been spending more time overseeing the razing of his damaged warehouse. Instead, all he wanted to do was see Emilia.

His wife.

When he thought of her, his chest grew tight. And so did his bloody breeches. Which was a hell of a thing when one was stepping over the threshold of one's home and handing off his hat and gloves to his butler.

"Do you know where I might find Mrs. Winter, Nash?" he asked the august domestic.

"I do believe Mrs. Winter is now resting in her chamber, Mr. Winter," Nash informed him.

Nash had been a butler to the Earl of Whitlock before Dev had hired him. Whitlock had gone pockets to let, and Dev had pockets that were exceedingly deep. Endless, in fact. Dev had found Nash by a grand stroke of fortune, all the better to increase his stature. He had the best domestics anyone could afford. And now, he had a wife who was the daughter of a duke. His sisters would soon make excellent matches beneath her intelligent tutelage, of that he had no doubt.

The one thing he had craved but which had been forever out of reach would soon be his.

"Thank you, Nash," he said.

His feet were already moving before he had finished his sentence. By his own admission, his plan of giving Emilia time and allowing her to come to him—aside from the scalding interlude in his study—had failed. In the days following her rejection, he had told himself all manner of stories meant to ameliorate the damage.

He stalked toward the staircase, intending to take the steps two at a time, all the faster to reach her. He had stayed away long enough. As long as he could tolerate, damn it. And he could not bear to allow any more time to pass without seeing her. He would see her this day, this hour, this minute.

"Dev, there you are!"

The feminine exclamation did not belong to his wife. Of course it did not. Why would Emilia deign to refer to him in such an intimate fashion? She was too busy pining for Edgeworth.

He turned, gritting his teeth against the reminder of his wife's dead betrothed, to find his youngest sister, Bea sweeping toward him. He offered her a polite bow.

She curtseyed. "I was hoping I could speak with you."

"If this is about the damned *accoucheur*, the answer is still *no*," he bit out. Ordinarily, he made certain he possessed a great deal of patience for his youngest sister.

Not today.

Today, his wife had run him to the bone. He had no more tolerance for Bea's escapades. After spending time at the foundling hospital he funded, Bea had decided she wished to become a midwife. All whilst he was attempting to make the

Winters a respectable family. If he had his way, every one of his sisters would marry well.

The gentlemen in question would need to care for his sisters. They would also need to prove themselves to him. But he was in the business of expanding the Winter empire, not undermining it. And the notion of his youngest sister engaged in midwifery…it was untenable.

"But Dev," his sister pleaded. "I have already explained to you, I have no wish to wed a lord as you insist I must do. Emilia agrees with me. She says I ought to be able to choose the path I wish to follow."

His gaze narrowed upon his wayward minx of a sister. "Indeed? Is that what Lady Emilia told you?"

"Yes." Bea's cheeks went red. "She said she was denied the right to choose her own course, and she knows better than anyone how very difficult it is."

Christ.

Is that what she believed? He had courted her for *weeks*. Yes, he had bought up her father's vowels in an effort to influence her decision. The businessman in him could not so easily be sweetened into a gentleman, after all. But he had done everything in his power to make certain their marriage had been Lady Emilia's choice.

"Are you certain that is what Lady Emilia told you?" he demanded.

Bea's eyes widened at the strength of his tone, and he could not blame her, for whilst he was a coldhearted bastard in business, he was softhearted when it came to his sisters. He would give them anything within his means, as long as he deemed it in their best interests.

And he did not damn well consider his youngest, innocent, *unwed* sister aiding an *accoucheur* to be in her best interest.

"I…" Bea paused, seeming to collect herself. "Yes, Dev.

96

Emilia said I ought to follow my heart. My heart is not in becoming a lady. Surely you must see that. I want to do something useful. To do something meaningful. I am horrid at watercolors, and I cannot abide by needlework—"

"Enough," he interrupted coldly, silencing her when she would have continued to plead her case. He did not want to think about Bea's complaints now. Not after she had just revealed his wife still believed he had forced her into wedding him. "You are young, Bea. You cannot decide your life now. Grant yourself time. Do not rush to do anything foolhardy. Becoming a midwife will ruin you in the eyes of society. If the Winters are ever to escape our common heritage, we must do it ourselves, with our wits."

"Is that why you married Lady Emilia?" Bea asked. "Was it only so you could secure a noble bride? Did you not care for her at all? Did you truly force her to marry you?"

Jesus. When had his youngest sister become such a woman? Why was she so defiant, glaring at him, demanding things of him, becoming just as headstrong and as trouble-some as her four elder sisters?

He did not have to answer her insolent questions. He was the head of the Winter family, *by God*, and she had no right to question him. No right to take a stand against him, to demand things of him he could not give her.

Except, if her questions were also Emilia's questions…

He swallowed. "I did not force Lady Emilia to marry me."

But he had not been fair either, had he? Like every busi-ness dealing he had ever undertaken, he had made certain for his negotiations with Lady Emilia, he possessed all the power. All the ability to bargain. To get what he wanted.

Namely, her.

Lady Emilia King had been a determined spinster, her heart on her sleeve, in love with her dead betrothed, when he had bought her father's vowels. She had never stood a chance against a determined Devereaux Winter. He was a man who undercut his business rivals without a thought. There was no room for emotion in business.

Fuck.

He was an utter bastard, wasn't he?

Lady Emilia was not a business matter. She was personal. *Very* personal.

"Good," Bea said then, sending a hesitant smile his way. "I would not like to think ill of my beloved brother."

She ought to think ill of him. He was beginning to think ill of himself.

"What do you think of Lady Emilia?" he asked Bea suddenly, on a whim.

To the best of his knowledge, his new wife had been getting on well with his sisters. She had been dutifully attending fittings, taking them shopping, and planning a massive house party, including a ball that would announce the places of all the Winters in high society.

"I admire her greatly," his sister told him, smiling. "You chose an excellent bride, Dev. She hardly seems like the lady you warned us she would be."

Ah, yes. Ruefully, he recalled the manner in which he had initially described Lady Emilia King to his sisters. But she had been cold and aloof then, the disapproving duke's daughter. Haughty and forbidding. How could he have known there was more to her, far more, than the icy aristocrat she had shown him?

"She is unparalleled," he told Bea before he reminded himself—quite sternly—about the midwifery nonsense. "But even Lady Emilia would no doubt tell you that a lady cannot be a midwife. The nonsense with the *accoucheur* needs to stop, Bea."

She bowed her head. "Yes, Dev."

Because he knew his sister, he doubted her sudden acceptance of his decree.

But because he also needed to see his wife, he was willing to accept Bea's response.

For now.

"I want the best for you," he added, guilt pricking him for reasons he could not entirely comprehend.

"You want what you deem is best for me," Bea returned, her tone stubborn and sad in equal measures. "That is the difference."

"Mayhap I know what is best for you better than you do," he pointed out. "I am ten years your senior, the oldest of all of us."

"Age does not necessitate wisdom," Bea told him sadly.

His youngest sister was right. He was not nearly as wise as he had hoped. "I love you, Bea," he told her. If she had been a lad, he would have called her a rapscallion, and he would have been right.

"And I love you, Dev." She paused, sending him a strange look. "I also love my new sister. I think you may as well."

Nay. He did not. He could not.

He refused to think it.

Had he fallen in love with Emilia?

Bloody hell.

What if he had?

CHAPTER 10

$\mathcal{E}$milia was about to ring for her maid to dress her for dinner when there was a tap at the door adjoining her chamber to her husband's. Following her bath, she had donned a dressing gown and had spent some time attempting to distract herself with her correspondence.

But had failed miserably.

Her mind and her heart were equally heavy, beset by questions.

The diversion she had so desperately sought could not be achieved, no matter how hard she tried. Instead, she had been occupying herself by pacing the floor and reminding herself of all the reasons why she should not trust a man like Devereaux Winter. All the reasons why she should fight to keep him at bay.

Now, it would seem the object of her troubled musings had arrived home uncharacteristically early. And he had sought her out. She glanced down at herself, painfully aware of her state of dishabille.

"Emilia," came his deep, decadent voice.

She suppressed a shiver. She could either send him away,

or she could bid him to enter. There was a choice to be made. Or was there? He was her husband, after all. He had every right.

"Enter," she called.

The door opened, and there he stood, dominating the threshold with his massive form. Had she ever thought him beastly and uncouth? A barbarian? It was impossible to imagine so as her gaze drifted over him, drinking in his masculine beauty.

His dark hair was too long and untamable, much like the man himself. His shoulders were wide and strong, his thighs encased in dark breeches today, which matched his waistcoat. His cravat was snowy white. He was all male, a collection of hard angles and sharp planes. His brown eyes traveled over her like a caress.

She tightened the belt securing her robe in place, unaccountably nervous. "Mr. Winter, you are home earlier than expected."

He bowed to her with fluid elegance. He was not wearing a coat, and the sight of his muscled arms in nothing but his shirtsleeves took her breath. "I adjourned my day early so I could join my lovely wife and sisters for dinner. I trust you are not displeased?"

Feeling foolish, she offered him an abbreviated curtsy as he strode inside her chamber. "Of course not. This is your home, Mr. Winter. You are free to come and go as it pleases you."

"This is your home now as well, Emilia," he said softly. "I hope you feel that way by now."

Did she?

She pondered that for a moment, watching him as he strode toward her, making her heart kick into a gallop. "I do."

The realization surprised her. She had not expected to feel as if she belonged here. Nor had she anticipated the depth of connection she would feel with the Winters. The Winter standing before her included.

He gifted her with one of his rare smiles, his dimples appearing and diminishing the harshness of his countenance. "I am glad to hear it."

The air seemed to hang, heavy and thick around them. Or perhaps that was the anticipation. Possibility beckoned her. She was achingly aware of her nakedness beneath her robe. Of the heat pouring from his big body in tempting waves.

"Thank you," she hastened to say before she did something foolish, like launch herself into his arms. "I visited my mother today, and she told me about Mr. Rhodes."

Was it her imagination, or did a slight tinge of red color his cheekbones?

"You need not offer me thanks. Securing Mr. Rhodes was a selfish act on my part." His voice was gruff.

She raised a brow, studying his handsome face. Yes, she was certain the impassive Devereaux Winter was flushing. "Selfish?"

He ran a hand over his jaw. "Yes. Buying up your father's vowels is damned expensive."

It was plain to see he was wallowing in discomfort at the notion she viewed him as compassionate. But there was more, far more, to Devereaux Winter than she had ever previously imagined. She knew that now. Just as she knew beneath his stern exterior beat a tender heart.

"Thank you all the same," she said. "It makes me happy to know someone is aiding him, and my mother is quite relieved. Many would say Papa is mad, but he is not. His mind is merely muddled. Some days, he is like himself, and other days, it is as if a fog claims him."

"The mind can be a strange beast, and age and infirmity do not affect all in the same manner." He paused, frowning.

"There is something I must speak to you about, Emilia. An apology I must make."

He took her hands in his then, and warmth blossomed in her belly. Wherever her skin touched his, she burned. Yearning slid through her as she recalled the way he had made her feel, his mouth upon her most sensitive flesh...

She forced the memory from her mind. Her wanton body was already playing tricks upon her. No need to further her weakness for him.

"What apology must you make?" she asked.

"More than one," he began, his jaw clenching as he paused, seeming to search for the proper words. "But I will begin here: I am sorry I put my needs above your own when I pursued our marriage. I am a selfish bastard, Emilia, and ruthless, and a scoundrel. I am everything my reputation says I am, and worse. All I could think about was what I wanted, what I needed, and when I saw the opportunity to buy your father's debts and use them to my advantage, I did, never once thinking of you. Never once thinking about what you wanted, what you needed."

His words shocked her and against her better judgment, touched her. Devereaux Winter's capacity to surprise her seemed endless. "You warned me you were ruthless, Mr. Winter. I expected nothing less."

But instead, he had not been ruthless at all. He had been compassionate. Tender. Almost endearing. She had never been more confused. But her husband was not done with his apologia yet, for he continued.

"I cannot change what has happened, or undo what has already been done, but I can promise you it will never happen again." His gaze was intense, boring into hers. "I vow to you that I will always put your needs and wants before mine, from this moment onward."

No one, not even James, had ever made such a pledge to her before.

She searched her husband's face for signs of prevarication and saw none. He appeared nothing but earnest. His countenance was stark and open, awaiting her rejection or her forgiveness.

Emilia understood how much his admission would have cost him. He was a proud man. Strong. Unyielding. Something inside her shifted. Changed. Tears pricked her eyes, and for a few poignant beats, she could not speak. Could do nothing save stand there, staring at him, holding on to his hands as if he alone could rescue her from the raging floodwaters of her past.

And perhaps it was true.

"You need not say anything," he said. "You need not forgive me or believe me. I will prove myself to you. This, I swear."

For so many years, she had felt as if she were broken, on the inside. Lost without James. Lost without his love and the life they were meant to have together. Now, for the first time, she began to feel as if healing—as if becoming whole again—was a possibility for her.

There was only one response she could have, and she gave it to him now. "I trust you. And I forgive you. I forgive you, Dev."

His eyes darkened at her use of his name. He brought her hands to his lips, placing a reverent kiss upon each of them. "Thank you, Emilia."

A swift current of longing rushed through her. How she wanted him to kiss her. But this was new, unfamiliar territory between them. She scarcely knew how to act when they were not at odds with each other.

"I promise to also put your needs and wants before mine,"

she said instead of begging for his mouth upon hers. "Our union ought to be an even trade, should it not?"

His gaze flicked to her lips, then settled back upon hers. "If you insist, I shall not argue."

"I insist." Her nipples tightened, and her breasts felt heavy beneath his molten regard.

He brought her hands to his lips for another kiss atop each one, and then, his eyes never leaving hers, he flipped them upside down, revealing the pale undersides of her wrists. One by one, he pressed his lips there, over her throbbing pulse.

He inhaled, the blade of his nose against her skin. "You smell sweet, like flowers. I trust you found the soap?"

"Yes." She shivered when he nudged the sleeve of her robe higher, allowing his lips greater access. He kissed a path of fire along her arm. "You changed the recipe according to my suggestions."

"When Mrs. Winter speaks, I listen." He smiled against her skin.

One of his dimples reappeared.

The breath rushed from her lungs.

The ache inside her could no longer be contained.

"Dev," she whispered.

He stilled, lowering her hands and lifting his head. "Emilia?"

"If you do not kiss me now, I shall go mad with wanting," she burst out.

His grin deepened. *Dear heavens*, but he was a gorgeous creature.

And this gorgeous creature was *hers*. A stab of possession she had never felt before hit her then.

"Then you leave me with no choice, darling." With one yank of her hands, he hauled her body to his. They were flush, thigh to thigh, chest to chest, mouths a scant distance apart. "I shall have to kiss you."

And then he did.

* * *

Dev groaned as his mouth moved over his wife's. She was sweet and soft and giving. His hands found her waist, then glided lower until he cupped her delectable rump. Though he tried his best to temper the kiss, the desire for her he had been controlling with rigid determination over the last few months finally snapped.

There was no control any longer.

There was only Emilia, covered in a thin, smooth dressing gown, kissing him back as if she were starved for him. With two hands full of her derriere, he moved her more firmly against him, grinding his stiff cock into the softness of her belly.

He had not intended for his apology to turn into an opportunity for him to make love to her, but now that she was in his arms where she belonged, there was no way in hell he was letting her go. He deepened the kiss, his tongue slipping into the honeyed depths of her mouth. And she responded in kind, making a throaty feminine growl and running her tongue along his.

Her hands were in his hair, and Christ, he loved the feeling of her touching him. Of her tongue moving against his. Of her body pressed into him. He had waited. And waited. He had all but worn his cock raw lying in bed next door, thinking of her so close and yet so far away. Beyond his reach. But she was decidedly not beyond his reach now.

Something between them had changed, irrevocably.

He had felt it, an indistinct heaviness, hanging in the air from the moment he had first entered her chamber. And it had only grown more pronounced. He finally felt, for the first time since their initial meeting, they had reached an understanding. There was no resentment in her touch, no hesitation. Only the same hunger and need raging through him. He was far from perfect, but for her sake, and for the sake of their union, he wanted to be better. He wanted to be the husband she deserved.

But more than anything, he wanted to become her husband in truth.

In deed and not just vows.

He broke the kiss, giving her rump a tender squeeze. "Emilia, I—"

She stayed his words by pressing a finger to his lips. "Yes."

There it was again, his favorite word, in her melodious voice.

His ballocks tightened, and a wave of lust rolled down his spine. But he was compelled to act the gentleman. Even if it nearly killed him.

He kissed her finger, then removed it from his lips. "You do not know what you are agreeing to."

"I do." Her eyes searched his, and instead of retreating, she caressed the side of his face. "You asked me if you could come to me four days ago in your study, and I should have told you 'yes' then. I am telling you now."

Hell and damnation. There was nothing he could do but kiss her again. And again. It was soon time to dress for dinner, but dinner could go hang for all he cared. But then, it occurred to him he did not wish to pressure or influence her in any way. Though their desire was clearly mutual, the last thing he wanted was to rush her into sharing his bed.

He broke the kiss. "This has to be your decision, Emilia. I

will wait. We have the rest of our lives together. There is no need to make this choice in haste."

She shook her head. "I do not want to wait, Dev."

Her lips were dark and swollen with his kisses, the pupils of her eyes dilated wide with pleasure. He had never seen a more lovely sight. He kissed her again. Slowly. Lingeringly. Taking his time. He worked his mouth over hers, teased the fullness of her lower lip with a nip.

He dragged his lips from hers with great effort. Releasing her bottom with the same reluctance, he took her hands in his and began pulling her across her chamber, walking them both to his. If they were going to consummate their union at last, it was going to happen in his chamber. In his bed.

He wanted her scent on his bedclothes, her naked in the same place where he had so vividly imagined her. This time, she would be flesh-and-blood rather than a chimera.

"Where are we going?" she protested, her expression dazed, her tone confused.

"To my bed," he told her. "Where you belong."

Where she had *always* belonged.

And Lord help anyone who attempted to stand in his way.

CHAPTER 11

*E*milia gripped her husband's hands tightly, allowing him to lead her through the door joining their chambers, past their shared dressing area, to his chamber. When they reached it, she resisted the urge to stop, turn around, and run like a frightened doe back to the safety of her chamber.

Entering his domain for the first time made what she was about to do far more real.

She had never before seen the interior of his chamber. *Oh*, she had been tempted to peek on more than one occasion. But she never had. The interior was spacious and elegantly—if sparsely—decorated.

She would have expected from a man of his immense wealth more ostentation, more gilt. But the walls were hung with muted blue coverings, and the paintings enhancing it were not at all effusive. Rather, they were understated pastoral oils in bleak tones. His bed was large and harsh and solid-looking, taking up most of the far wall. Rather symbolic, she thought, of the man who slept within it.

Aside from the bed, there was a writing desk, a chest of

drawers, and a bedside table. The rugs were thick and extravagant, just as the carpeting in her chamber was. But she could not help but to notice the simplicity of his chamber. The sparseness of it.

He was a man who continually surprised her. Who confounded her. Who bemused her...

He led her all the way to the bed before he stopped, just short of it. His dark eyes singed her to her soul. "You are certain?"

Was she?

She could scarcely breathe.

Her heart was thumping, her entire body aflame, aching for him. Needing him. She was terrified of him and desperate for him all at once. But she knew what she wanted, and it was her husband. It was Devereaux Winter.

Dev.

Of the way he made her feel, she was utterly certain. Of the wisdom of what she was about to do? Not nearly as much. But she also knew the time had come. She was ready. She wanted to know him, to be as close to him as she could be. To understand him, if she could, even in a small way.

"Yes." She flicked her tongue over her bottom lip. "I am certain."

"Thank fuck." His crude language shocked her.

The word was a forbidden one, but when Devereaux Winter spoke it in his deep, delicious voice, she *liked* it.

And in the next instant, she forgot to be shocked. Indeed, she forgot everything but the sensation of her husband's mouth on hers. Then on her throat. Of his fingers finding the knot on her dressing gown and plucking it open. The silken fabric fell from her shoulders in a whispered hush to the floor. She was nude before him, but she was not cold. Not ashamed.

Instead, she was on fire. She needed more of him, every

part of him. She wanted his skin. Longed to explore the sinews and strength of his frame. Emilia's fingers found the buttons of his waistcoat. One by one, she tore them open. She did it as she kissed him. As their lips and tongues meshed.

The waistcoat was gone. He kissed a path down her throat. She wanted his shirt gone too. It was fine lawn, but it wasn't *him*. She wanted nothing between them. She wanted Devereaux Winter with a ferocity that made her tremble, that shook her to her core.

She grasped handfuls of his shirt and pulled it up. He aided her, and together, they dragged it over his head, leaving his torso bared for her exploration. She took a moment first to admire him. If his chest had seemed wide and immovable, a veritable wall beneath the trappings of civility, he appeared somehow even larger without them. His chest was well delineated, stippled with a fine smattering of masculine dark hair. But it was the size of him—massive, muscled, so very strong—which took her breath most.

Emilia dared to lay a palm against his flesh. His heat scalded her as his muscles rippled beneath her tentative touch. Nothing could have prepared her for the reality of him, the barely leashed power. Or the way he made her feel, struck with desperation. With need.

She wanted to say something, but her tongue would not cooperate. Her hands were too busy learning the taut planes of his body, claiming him as surely as he had claimed her. When his mouth moved back to hers, none of that mattered anyway. His lips moved, claiming and possessive. She opened for him.

His tongue was in her mouth. His scent was all she breathed in. His smooth, firm body taunted her traveling fingertips, lured her for more.

More, always more.

And he gave her more, too. His hands cupped her breasts, his fingers working her hard nipples into distended peaks. He pinched, then rolled them between thumb and forefinger. The throbbing between her legs bloomed into an ache. She needed him there. Needed his touch, the melting surge of release.

Her hunger for him turned voracious. But not just hungry. Rather, demanding. It was her turn to nip his lip, to catch the sensual fullness between her teeth and bite until he groaned. To send a tentative touch over the rigid protrusion in his breeches until the breath hissed from him.

"Slowly." His breathing was ragged, his eyes molten chocolate as they bored into hers.

Her hand was still upon him, and he felt so vital, so firm and long and strong, pulsing against her palm. She did not wish for slow. She wished for fast. For the unknown. He seemed to understand what she wanted, for he covered her hand with his, guiding her, showing her how to touch him.

"Feel what you do to me, Emilia," he said lowly.

Desire unfurled, potent and heady, as she curled her fingers around the length of him and stroked with his help. An answering ache began at the apex of her thighs, where he had brought her to the heights of pleasure with his mouth just days before. And then, as if he knew her body's needs better than she did, his hand left hers, and his fingers brushed over her.

Gently at first, skimming over her before parting her folds. His long fingers unerringly found the pulsing flesh hidden within. He toyed with the most sensitive part of her, and an exquisite bolt of bliss shot through her, beginning at her core and radiating outward.

Her lips found his. This time, their kiss was bruising. Scorching. He was thrusting against her hand, growing larger and thicker, it seemed, by the heartbeat. And she was already on the brink of achieving the same crescendo she had reached before. And she wanted it. Oh, how she wanted it, with a greed that would not be denied.

Her hips moved instinctively against his hand as she sucked on his tongue. He increased the pressure, working over her nub until her entire body seized and a decadent paroxysm took her. She cried out into his mouth, shuddering against him.

But it was not enough.

He severed the kiss on a groan, his fingers leaving her throbbing flesh to work upon the fall of his breeches. Her need for him had only grown. She could not stop touching him, kissing him. Her mouth worshiped his bare chest, the protrusion of his collarbone, his corded neck.

Finally, his breeches were gone. He caught her waist in his big hands and lifted her onto the bed, following her, kissing everywhere. Her lips, the tip of her nose, her ear, down her throat to her shoulder, her nipple, and then lower still, his teeth nipping in little love bites over her skin, alternating with the kisses.

He made his way to the jut of her hip bone, where he bit, then licked. He caressed her, and she parted her legs, wanting him there. Wanting his touch, his tongue. Once more, he seemed to know her body's silent pleas. He kissed her inner thigh, settled his massive body between her legs, and lowered his head.

It was wicked, she knew, and she ought to close her eyes or look away, but Emilia had never seen a more erotic sight than Dev delivering hot little kisses to her mound. He moaned into her, as if she were the most decadent sweet and he could not help but to indulge. When his tongue glided hotly over the turgid bud hidden within her folds, she cried out, her body bowing from the bed.

"So perfect," he murmured against her skin. "Do you like what I am doing to you, Emilia?"

He sucked.

"Yes." She was breathless with desire. Her entire body was wound tight.

Tenderly, he ran his tongue over her in a procession of soft, fluttering licks. "Tell me." He sucked again, then used his teeth. "Say my name."

Her fingers were in the thick, inky profusion of his hair. Sensation overwhelmed her. She did not think she even had the power to speak. She writhed against his mouth, her body overcoming her mind in its desperate need for more of her husband's skilled sensual torture.

He lifted his head, then blew a stream of hot air over her folds. "My name. I want to hear it."

She would give him anything he wanted. Anything. Everything. As long as he did not stop. "Dev," she gasped, arching against him. "Please, Dev."

He gave her what she wanted, drawing her back into his mouth. One pull was all she needed. She shattered, and it was his name on her lips, his big body drawing over hers as the ripples of euphoria still rocked her.

She framed his beautiful face in her hands as he settled himself between her legs, spreading them even wider. His mouth was glistening with her essence, and his shaft was thick and hard against her core.

He kissed her, the taste of her on his lips. She kissed him back, wrapping her arms around his neck. She lost herself then. She became someone else, someone brave and defiant and unfettered. The ties between the woman she had believed herself to be and the woman she had become broke. In his arms, in his kiss, in his bed, she was new again.

He was all she wanted, wicked and wild.

She rolled her hips, seeking more contact, clinging to him

as his fingers delved between them, dipping into her folds, stroking her. Her every sense was so heightened by the two releases he had already given her that she feared she would come undone again with nothing more than his touch.

He kissed down her jaw, to her ear. "I need to be inside you, Emilia. I will be as gentle as I can."

The first time, there would be pain. Mama had warned her. It was difficult to believe in the wake of such tremendous pleasure. But she was beyond the point of caring. Her thoughts were jumbled. Everything had changed, and nothing, nothing would ever be the same.

She turned her head, her mouth seeking his. On a groan, he deepened the kiss, plundering, taking. His fingers moved, stroking her. Teasingly, he swirled around her entrance. Just when she thought she would go mad with waiting and needing, his shaft replaced his fingers. The firm length of him glanced over her aching flesh.

Frustrated at the slow torture, she ended the kiss, her breathing harsh and ragged as she met his gaze with hers. "Now, Dev. I cannot wait."

"Damn," he growled. "I am trying not to hurt you."

"Do it," she whispered.

The new Emilia was brazen, her body ruling her mind. The pain would fade, but this longing would not. All she wanted was his claiming. His touch. Him, deep inside her. There was only one way to quell the hunger raging inside her.

He moved then, giving them both what they wanted. He slid inside her, and the sensation was exquisite. She was terrified and exhilarated all at once. Her hands found his shoulders, her nails sinking deep into his muscles. His face was a study in concentration. He kissed her, thrusting at the same time.

A twinge of pain sliced through her. She was stretched,

full of him. He kissed his way down her neck, finding her breasts. When he sucked a nipple, she could not hold herself still. She bucked, bringing him deeper. He made a low sound of masculine surrender and his hips pumped as he suckled her. She moved with him as they found a rhythm. Slowly, the sting of his possession eased.

One more thrust, and he was seated inside her completely.

No other sensation could compare to the feeling of him like this, within her, a part of her. They were joined. He was hers, and she was his. Tenderly, he kissed a path back to her mouth. He guided her legs around his waist, before his fingers found her once more.

He began moving in earnest then, in and out, faster. The friction proved even more wondrous, and when his fingers stroked the plump bud of her sex, she lost all control. An intense burst of sensation rushed over her. She clenched on him, clutching him to her as the waves broke over her, persistent as the sea.

"Emilia," he whispered against her lips, as if her name were a prayer.

He rocked into her, his big body stiffening. A warm rush entered her, and she gasped, a fresh series of spasms over-taking her as they lost themselves together. In that heart-pounding moment, they became one.

CHAPTER 12

*B*edding his wife had rotted his mind.

Dev was certain of it.

That was the reason he was escorting her to the theater for the third time in less than a fortnight. She was seated opposite him in the carriage, dressed to perfection in a blue gown that set off her startling eyes to perfection. From her ears, throat, and hair gleamed the sapphire and diamond parure he had gifted her two days before.

Or perhaps it was that he was besotted with her.

Yes, he was most definitely besotted with Emilia. How could he not be?

Since consummating their marriage, they had fallen into an unspoken truce. She spent every night in his bed. And he spent every day whiling away the hours, plodding through his work, until he could return to her. He found himself relying on Merrick now more than ever, keeping shorter hours.

"You are frowning," his wife observed shrewdly. "Is something amiss?"

"Nothing at all," he said blandly. "I was merely admiring how lovely you are tonight, my dear."

In truth, he did not like being at her mercy. He was not certain he approved of the changes she wrought in him. They terrified him, truth be told. And with each day that passed, he became increasingly convinced his youngest sister was right, that he had lost his heart to Emilia.

He gritted his teeth at the thought as the remembrance of her earlier words returned. *I do not love you, Mr. Winter. My heart belongs to another.* Could her heart ever be his? He had won over her body, these past few weeks, but he was beginning to fear that wasn't enough.

That he wanted more. That he, in turn, had more to give her.

"I find it difficult to believe you are admiring me when your countenance is as ferocious as a thundercloud," she quipped then. "Will you not tell me what has overset you?"

"I was merely thinking about the final stage of rebuilding my warehouse," he fibbed, not about to disclose the embarrassingly maudlin content of his thoughts to her.

"You are certain?" she sounded suspicious.

His wife was intelligent. It was just one of the many traits he had found to admire in her. "And wondering at the wisdom of attending the theater for the third time in the last fortnight."

A soft smile curved her mouth. "Thank you for escorting me."

His ears went hot under her tender regard. He cleared his throat. "I was not otherwise occupied."

Her lips twitched. "Of course."

Was the impertinent female laughing at him?

He swore she was. And how laughable that in itself was—a small slip of a woman, less than half his size, laughing at a man whom so many feared.

"What is so humorous, Mrs. Winter?" he could not help but to ask.

"The expression on your face, Mr. Winter," she replied with a cheeky grin. "You are trying so very hard to be gruff, and yet with me you are always tender and sweet. Gentler than a lamb."

She was goading him, and he knew it. But he could not resist the temptation she presented. "Gentler than a lamb, am I?"

"Dev," she protested, her eyes going wide.

But it was too late. He was feeling rather wicked. He reached across the interior of the carriage, caught her waist in his hands, and lifted her onto his lap. "Emilia," he said, kissing her throat where her pulse beat. "Do not tempt me to show you how very unlike a lamb I am."

She moved in his lap, settling the delectable curves of her rump more firmly against his already hard cock. Her arms went around his neck. "What if I want you to show me?" she whispered.

"Damn it, Emilia." The last thing he wanted to do was fuck his wife in their carriage *en route* to the theater.

Then again, he had never taken a woman in a carriage before, and she was so damn beautiful, her lips begging for a kiss. He wondered if she was wet. A glance out the window to ascertain their surroundings proved they had a few minutes—ten or more—until they reached their destination.

She pressed her mouth to his neck, just below his ear. "Perhaps I can help to distract you from your warehouse."

Christ, she could distract him from anything and everything with no effort whatsoever on her part. But if she kept kissing his neck and moving suggestively in his lap as she was, he was going to spend in his breeches.

"What do you have in mind?" he asked thickly, positioning her so that she was astride him, her gown billowing around them.

He could not resist skimming a hand up her inner thigh, straight to her cunny. She was soaked, her folds slick and hot and ready. They both groaned as he slid a finger inside her. She gripped him, grinding against him, seeking more.

She may still be in love with a ghost, but he was the man she wanted, *thank God*. He would take whatever she was willing to give. As much of her as he could get. With his thumb, he worked her pearl, stroking the swollen nub until she shuddered and cried out, coming undone in his arms.

But he was not through yet. Withdrawing from her, he undid the fall of his breeches. His cock sprang free, aching and ready. He kissed her, doing his best to keep from destroying her coiffure. It would not do to arrive at the theater with a wife who looked as if she had been ravished in the carriage on the way to their destination.

Even if it was true.

"I want you inside me, Dev," she said.

It was all the prodding he needed. He guided her down upon his rigid length, sliding home in one swift thrust. Hot wetness kissed his shaft. She clenched on him, moaning. Damn, but she undid him. She was all he could think, all he could see, all he could feel.

Nothing but Emilia.

They moved together, both greedy, both hungry, each wanting the release only the other could give. Her rhythm was halting at first, but as she gained confidence, she moved faster, taking him deeper, and he knew he was not going to last. They fucked with a ferocity that had him grinding his teeth to hold his climax at bay.

"Take what you want," he told her.

And she did. Small, breathy moans escaped her as she slammed down upon his prick again and again. Her channel squeezed him like a fist. So hot. So wet. So tight. So bloody good. He parted her cloak and tugged down her bodice and chemise, revealing her breasts. They bounced as she fucked him, her pert little nipples hard against the cool air of the autumn night. He bent his head and feathered his tongue over first the left, then the right, leaving them glistening.

She moaned, riding him faster.

He kissed the curve of her breast, feeling the powerful swelling of his own climax rising. "I want to suck your nipples while you come on my cock."

As always, his coarse words drove his wife closer to the edge. She moaned, a rush of moisture bathing his length. When he suckled the peak of her breast, she tightened on him, trembling as her release washed over her. And he was not far behind, jerking his hips upward, pounding into her sweet heat. He came inside her so hard, white stars burst before his vision.

When she collapsed against him, her heart pounding into his, he was breathless and boneless both. He kissed the tip of her nose, thinking again of how beloved she was to him. How very necessary.

How much she terrified him.

But then, he pushed all those unwanted feelings and thoughts aside.

"Feel free to distract me any time you wish, wife," he told her.

* * *

"Lady Merton wishes to call upon you, Mrs. Winter," Nash informed Emilia.

She paused in the midst of her needlework to consider

the butler's announcement. The Viscountess Merton was not a familiar of Emilia's. They had never traveled in the same circles, and her fast reputation meant she was not the sort of lady with whom Emilia's mother would allow her to associate. That Lady Merton would call upon her now seemed odd indeed.

Especially since she had noticed the elder woman casting longing glances in the direction of her husband last night at the theater. Although Dev had not appeared to notice, when Emilia had pointed it out to him, he had looked distinctly uncomfortable, his tone growing clipped.

"She is not anyone you ought to concern yourself with, my dear," he had said simply, and that had been that.

But now, the lady in question had come to call. Emilia did not believe it was a coincidence. Misgiving burned in her belly, but so too did curiosity. And something else, an emotion far more foreign: jealousy.

"Shall I tell her ladyship you are not at home?" Nash pressed helpfully.

Ordinarily, she would have agreed. But there had been something in the manner in which her husband had reacted to Lady Merton's presence last night that had left her troubled. That still left her troubled today.

"I will receive her," she decided. "Please show her in, Nash."

The butler bowed and left. The moment he was gone, Emilia wondered over the wisdom of her decision. Nothing good could come of her association with such a woman, surely. She thought once more of the glances the beautiful, golden-haired Lady Merton had sent toward Dev, of the shockingly low cut of her décolletage.

But before she could further consider the matter, the lady herself appeared. At such proximity, the viscountess was even more beautiful than Emilia had supposed. Her golden curls were artfully arranged to frame her face while more locks were swept into a chignon. Her bold red day gown was cut to accentuate her ample curves and large bosom. Everything about her was sultry, and Emilia knew a punishing rush of inadequacy as they exchanged polite greetings.

By contrast, Emilia was dark-haired, plain, and lacking all the voluptuousness Lady Merton possessed in abundance. Instead, her frame was rather thin and shapeless. When her husband had mockingly referred to her as a waif upon their first meeting, he had not been far off the mark.

If a creature such as this was interested in Devereaux Winter, Emilia could not compare. The knowledge made her spine straighten and a touch of bitterness creep into her voice when she spoke at last.

"Lady Merton, I am surprised at your call." Best not to dally with words, she decided, but to confront the beast. Besides, they were not acquaintances, and after the manner in which the viscountess had gazed longingly upon Emilia's husband the evening before, she could not believe they would ever be friends.

"Are you, my dear?" Lady Merton flashed her a smile that struck Emilia as bright and insincere. "I am sorry if this meeting causes you discomfort, but since you are Dev's wife now, I thought it best that we should meet privately. It is considerably less awkward and upsetting for the both of us."

Dev. All she could think, as she grappled to understand what her unexpected caller had just said, was that the viscountess had called her husband *Dev*.

And she did not like it.

"Indeed?" She affected a cool smile of her own, for she would not allow Lady Merton to suppose she had the upper hand in this unspoken battle being waged between them. "I confess, I am confused as to why a meeting between us should prove either awkward or uncomfortable, as you suggest."

Lady Merton's golden eyebrows—as perfectly formed as the rest of her—arched. "Forgive me, Lady Emilia. After last night, I supposed Dev had informed you."

Icy fronds of dread unfurled within her. "What might *Mr. Winter* have informed me of?" she asked, stressing the formality of her husband's name, for she did not think she could listen to the other woman call him Dev one more time whilst remaining civil.

Lady Merton pressed a gloved hand over her lips, as if she were stunned by the revelation. Emilia could not shake the impression the viscountess was feigning, but perhaps her dislike of the woman was coloring her judgment.

"My dear, this is a delicate matter," she said. "My sole intent in paying you this call was to tell you I understand your position. If you should need a confidante, I would be more than happy to be yours. It may seem disconcerting to share the affections of one's husband, but I assure you, in our set, it is more common than not."

The more Lady Merton spoke, the more a relentless tide of fury rose within Emilia. Sharing the affections of one's husband? Surely the supposed lady before her would not have the effrontery to suggest Dev had tender feelings for her?

"I am afraid I do not understand your implications, Lady Merton," she said stonily, her voice trembling with her barely suppressed anger.

"Oh dear." The viscountess's voice was hushed. "I am sorry, Lady Emilia. I thought you had discovered the truth. When Dev disappeared from your box to meet me, I assumed he had your approval. I ought not to have paid the whispers about you any heed. I see that now."

When Dev met her? Last night?

Emilia thought back to the previous evening. Her husband had indeed excused himself from the box for a few minutes. But he had returned immediately. She had not thought anything of it at the time, but in conjunction with Lady Merton's words, his actions suddenly held the taint of suspicion.

Fighting against a wave of nausea, she struggled to parse everything the viscountess had just said.

"You are suggesting my husband met you in secret last night whilst he escorted me to the theater, my lady?" she asked coldly.

"I am not suggesting, my dear." Although Lady Merton's tone was pitying, her countenance was smug. "He did. I am so sorry if you did not know. I never would have come here if I had realized. But the whispers about you...that you are frigid, that your heart belonged to Edgeworth, seemed to suggest the same story Dev told me."

"The story he told you," she repeated through numb lips.

Her husband had made love to her in the carriage on the way to the theater. And this creature was sitting before her now, suggesting he had then met *her* in secret, that she had some sort of relationship with him.

"He said he married you to aid his sisters in making matches with gentlemen," Lady Merton said.

The revelation cut more surely than any blade, because it was true. He had admitted as much himself before they had married. But it also hurt because she had imagined they had both surpassed their initial reasons for marrying each other. That they had grown to respect and desire each other.

"I suppose he did," she forced herself to say quietly, for she was determined not to allow the other woman to see how deeply she was affected.

"He could not marry me, of course, since I am already wed," Lady Merton said then, smiling again, before compressing her pout in a parody of compassion. "I would have offered to aid his sisters, but it would have been dreadfully inappropriate of me to act as their sponsors, given our understanding."

Lady Merton's insinuations, though thinly veiled, were clear. For the second time since Devereaux Winter had entered her life, Emilia knew the sickening realization of her entire world as she knew it changing irrevocably.

And she could not bear to listen to another moment of the other woman speaking.

She rose from her seat, forgetting everything but the defensive need to keep from hearing one more word. "You must go now, Lady Merton," she said, not caring for precedence or formality. "And do not call again. You are not welcome here at Dudley House."

Without bothering to offer so much as a curtsy, she sailed from the chamber, finding Nash and making certain he would escort her caller out. She made it all the way to her bedchamber before the tears claimed her.

But she did not allow them to claim her for long, because she was Lady Emilia King, and damn it all, though she may not have anything else, she had her pride.

* * *

Something was amiss.

Dev recognized it the moment a grave Nash accepted his hat, coat, and gloves when he returned to Dudley House that evening.

"Good evening, Nash," he greeted his butler. "The household seems frightfully quiet. Is something wrong with the Misses Winter?"

"No, sir."

"Lady Emilia?" he asked next, dreading the answer.

"Her ladyship had a visitor today which has caused some...upset," Nash imparted, his face as expressionless as ever.

"A visitor?" He frowned. "Who?"

"Lady Merton," Nash answered.

Alice. Bloody hell, was it not bad enough she had ambushed him last night at the theater? Now she had paid a call upon his wife? He had told her in no uncertain terms the evening before that he was done with her, cutting all ties.

"Lady Merton," he repeated, misgiving growing within him. "She called upon Lady Emilia alone, Nash?"

Nash inclined his head. "Yes, sir."

Fuck.

Alice was a part of his past, and one he was not particularly proud of. One he had been unable to shake. He ought to have known she would not stop at letters and accosting him at the theater. What the hell had she said to Emilia to upset her and to cause Nash to look as if he were preparing to attend a funeral rather than going about his usual daily tasks?

He nodded. "Thank you, Nash."

The man's loyalty and discretion were both mightily appreciated, and Dev made a note to reflect that in his domestic's salary. He stalked from the marbled entryway then, in a desperate search for Emilia.

His quest came to an abrupt halt when he saw his ashen-faced wife, dressed to enter the cool autumn evening, descending the staircase. He rushed forward when she attained the bottom, not bothering with niceties.

"Emilia," he said, reaching for her.

She shrugged away from his touch. "Do not, I beg you."

Her voice was icy and remote, reminiscent of the way she had spoken to him when they had first met. Only, this time was different. There was an edge, half sadness, half rage, which had been absent before.

"Where are you going?" he asked, settling for the answer instead of touching her.

Terrified of the answer.

"I am returning to my home," she said, her face expressionless. A blank mask.

Emilia had never looked at him with such dispassion. As if she were a ghost. Sickness churned within him. "This is your home, wife."

"No," she said bitingly. "It is not. Nothing made me more cognizant of that fact than today when your mistress paid me a visit."

Damn Alice straight to hell, the madwoman. "I do not have a mistress, Emilia."

Her lips tightened. "Did you meet with her last night in the theater?"

Christ, he would not lie to her. "Yes, but unintentionally. She accosted me, and when she did, I made certain to tell her to keep her distance from you."

Emilia gave a bitter laugh then, but there was no light in her eyes, no levity in her expression. Only acrimony. "How considerate of you to order your mistress to stay out of my sight. Thank you, Mr. Winter."

"I already told you, she is not my mistress," he bit out, infuriated by Alice's meddling.

He had told her to leave him alone in no uncertain terms. He had not answered one of her letters in six months. And yet she dared to dog him now, when he had everything to lose. Emilia was worth a thousand Alices, and she always would be.

"I saw the looks she sent you last night," Emilia said then. "And then she appeared here this afternoon, telling me she would have married you herself if not for the inconvenience of her husband. That but for your *under-standing*, she would have played matchmaker for your sisters."

"We no longer have an understanding, damn it." He raked a hand through his hair as desperation seized him. Emilia could not leave him. She meant far too much.

She was everything to him.

"No longer," his wife repeated. "Then you admit you were…she was…"

Shame washed over him. "In the past. Months ago now, Emilia, I swear it to you. Well before we were ever wed. Please, tell me what she said—"

"Ask her yourself," Emilia snapped, her eyes flashing with anger.

Her eyes were glistening. Tears?

"I have no wish to speak to her ever again," he said, and it was the complete truth. "I am asking you."

"How dare you?" Her lip curled in the perfect, aristocratic sneer.

And then, before he could brace himself, the biting sting of her slap across his cheek rocked him. He rubbed his smarting cheek. *Christ*, but for a little wisp of a woman, she had strength. Then again, it was one of the many traits he admired about her.

"Emilia, please," he tried again.

"I will not repeat a word your paramour spoke," she bit out. "She said more than enough."

"She is not my paramour," he argued, frustration building within him. "You are my wife, damn it."

"I almost believed," she whispered, looking stricken. "For a moment, you had me, Mr. Winter. But I am not anything more than another business proposition for you, am I? I served a purpose. You bought me, you married me, and in return, I was to launch your sisters, secure their matches.

And meanwhile, you could make a fool of me with the beautiful Lady Merton."

"No, damn it."

That was not the way of it. Not at all. How could she possibly believe anything between them could be so simple, so easily explained? How could she think, for a moment, he was not consumed by her? That he did not want her more than he wanted his next breath?

"Make a fool of someone else, Devereaux Winter," she seethed. "I never want to see you again."

CHAPTER 13

a solid sennight.

One day turned into two.

And three. Then all the way to bloody seven, *and still*, Dev knocked on the door of the house next door to his, asking to see his wife. And Grimes denied him. Every. Godforsaken. Time.

Lady Emilia is not at home.

Lady Emilia is suffering from a megrim.

Lady Emilia has a lung infection.

Lady Emilia is paying calls.

Lady Emilia is once more not at home, Mr. Winter.

I am sorry, Mr. Winter, but Lady Emilia is not well.

On day seven, Dev knocked on the door with more force than necessary. He had already dealt with Lady Merton. He was confident he had convinced her to never again attempt to meddle with his marriage or his life. All it had required was the threat he would ruin Merton down to his last ha'penny, for Alice enjoyed her comfort whilst she cuckolded her husband. He had also urged her to write a confessional and send it, posthaste, to Emilia.

Whether or not his wife would believe it, he could not say.

He could only hope.

And hope was also why, every day for seven days, he had appeared next door, requesting an audience with his wife. Hope and something else, an emotion far more profound. It had taken Emilia leaving him for him to realize how much she meant to him.

Each day, he returned. Each day, he was denied. Ignored. Rebuffed.

Like a scolded puppy, he would retreat next door.

But today, he had come with something more. Today, he had a plan. What he had was his best chance of making his wife understand just how much he loved her.

Yes, *loved* her, *bloody hell.*

Grimes answered the door, his expression bored. "Mr. Winter, I am afraid Lady Emilia is—"

"Expecting me," he said, shouldering his way past the august retainer.

"Mr. Winter," the butler sputtered.

Apparently that was not what the old fellow had been about to say.

But also, apparently, Dev did not give a proper goddamn.

"Where is she, Grimes?" he asked as he stalked into the entryway.

"In the salon, I believe, Mr. Winter, but I must say—"

"Nothing," he returned as he made his way toward the salon. "You must say nothing at all, Grimes."

* * *

Emilia was once more engaged in the distraction of

needlework—such pleasure in stabbing her needle through an unsuspecting textile—when the unmistakable baritone of her husband's voice reached her.

It had been a sennight since she had left him. And though he had returned each day since, she had effectively kept him at a distance, denying an audience with him. Of course, knowing Devereaux Winter as she did—or at least as she *thought* she had—she had understood he would not settle for an endless procession of false excuses.

And a part of her had to admit, his determination pleased her.

And another part of her had to acknowledge she had missed him.

But the rest of her—the rational part of her—knew she did not dare forgive him. Did not dare trust him.

Not after what she had discovered. After what he had revealed to her.

The sound of footsteps reached her now. And she knew who they belonged to. Heavy, rhythmic, laden with decision. With authority.

The door to the salon opened.

There he was. A towering wall of handsome man, strong, debonair, and everything she wished she did not want. How could he make her so weak for him, even as her heart still ached?

"Emilia," he said, his gaze connecting with hers.

For a beat, she forgot about all the reasons she had been maintaining a distance between them the last seven days. But then, she forced herself to recall all of it—the ugliness of Lady Merton's visit.

"Mr. Winter," she acknowledged coolly, standing and offering him a perfunctory curtsy.

How strange it was to meet again in such fashion, as if they were nothing more to each other than polite strangers, when the truth could not be further from it. In the aftermath of the hurt and betrayal of that awful day, she had realized she was in love with her husband. That her heart had not lost its ability to heal or to love again when James had died as she had feared it did.

"I know you are angry with me," he began.

"I am angry with myself," she corrected, for it was the truth.

How could she have fallen in love with him? And with such ease? How could he have betrayed her?

His lips compressed into a grim line, and curse her, but she recalled how those lips felt against hers, how they felt on every part of her body. The traitorous heat cascading through her could not be quelled, regardless of how hard she tried.

He moved toward her then, closing the distance separating them until he stood before her, imposing, handsome. Near enough to touch. His familiar scent hit her—his soap, and him. Dev.

Longing hit her.

She forced it down.

"I missed you, Emilia," he said softly.

Her foolish heart ached at his admission. If he had said anything else—if he had railed against her, demanded her return, she could have girded herself against him. But this tender onslaught... How was she to remain impervious?

"Why have you come?" she asked, forcing herself to remain stern. To remain strong.

"Do I need a reason?" His gaze scoured her face, as if he were committing it to memory. "You are my wife, and I have not seen you in a bloody week."

"You know why."

"Emilia, Lady Merton is not my mistress," he said lowly. "The only understanding between us is that she is to never speak to you again. If she so much as speaks your name in the wrong tone of voice, she will deeply regret it, believe me."

She wanted to believe him. Oh, how she wanted to.

"She told me you would have married her had she been free," she pressed.

Dev's jaw clenched, and he ran a hand over it. The sight of his long fingers, even obscured by gloves, did strange things to her. Unwanted things.

"Pure fiction on her part," he denied flatly. "I never would have married a woman like her. And nor, I suspect, would she have married a man like me."

She searched his countenance for signs of prevarication and found none. "Are you in love with her?"

Though she did not want to know the answer, she *had* to know. Her greatest fear, as the days of their separation had gone by, had become painfully clear. She was terrified she had fallen in love with a man who did not love her, a man who had already given his heart to another.

"Is that what you believe?" Dev took another step closer to her, reaching for her.

She shrugged away from his touch, knowing that if she succumbed, she would find it even more difficult to guard her heart as she must. "I know not what to believe. Tell me how I am meant to feel. How would you feel if you were in my place?"

"I would be bloody furious," he growled. "I do not blame you for your anger, nor do I deny your right to feel it. Loathe me if you must. But believe me when I assure you there is only one woman I have ever loved, and it is damn well not a conniving jade like Lady Merton."

She stilled as his words settled over her. Could it be that her own fears and insecurities had led her astray? That Lady Merton had manipulated her into believing the worst of Dev and sent her fleeing in a panicked effort to save her own pride and heart?

That Emilia had been wrong about Dev, yet again?

Hope, stupid, incipient hope, burst inside her. "Who is the woman?"

"Can you not see?" His expression changed, losing some of its harshness.

Emilia shook her head. "Of course I cannot. Why do you think I have spent the last sennight here instead of at Dudley House?"

He reached for her again, and this time she did not rebuff him. His hands settled upon her waist, finding their home. And it felt right, so right. She could not deny it.

"You," he said then.

One word.

Simple, really.

And yet, remarkable.

"Me," she repeated stupidly.

"I love you, Lady Emilia Winter." Dev tugged her against him, reminding her of how perfectly their bodies fit together. "I think I have loved you from the moment you called me a lowborn rogue here in this very salon."

She had called him that, had she not? Shame pricked her. How mistaken she had been, again and again.

Her hands found his shoulders, solid and firm. As always, his heat lit an answering fire within her. "If you love me, why did you not tell me so? Why would you allow me to believe the worst of you after Lady Merton's visit?"

"I tried to defend myself, but you did not want to hear it, Emilia," he said, looking upon her with such naked affection, something inside her melted. "And the truth is, if I were in your place, I would have believed the worst of me as well. I have not earned your love or your trust. If you grant me the chance, I promise you, I will win both. But I come to you prepared, Emilia. I cannot bear to be the source of your unhappiness."

He paused, releasing a heavy sigh before he continued. "You have two choices. Annulments are deuced difficult to procure, but if I violate the terms of our marriage contract, we can obtain one by citing fraud. I will do so if that is what you want. You would then be free to live your life as you wish, unencumbered by me, owing me nothing."

He was willing to give her up, to sacrifice their union and perhaps even the futures of his sisters for her happiness. The realization took her breath. Hope blossomed into something else. Something bolder and brighter and brimming with promise.

She cupped his jaw with her hand. "What is the other choice, Dev?"

"The other choice is that you come home with me." His gloved hand moved over hers. "I am not a perfect man by any means. I cannot change the mistakes I made in my past. But I can promise you I am the man who loves you. Even if you do not love me back, even if you can never find a place for me in your heart, I will always love you. Nothing and no one can change that."

"Oh Dev," she murmured, a surge of emotion so powerful hitting her, she trembled beneath its onslaught. "There is no choice to be made. I choose you and your love, because I love you too."

"You love me?" he asked, awe in his deep, velvet-smooth voice.

She nodded. "I do."

"Strange way of showing it, Mrs. Winter," he grumbled then. "Refusing to see me for an entire week."

"I could not bear to see you," she admitted. "It hurt too much. When I thought you had betrayed me with Lady Merton... But I was wrong. And I am so sorry, Dev."

He stopped further words with his mouth. Those wicked lips of his settled over hers in a kiss that was deep and passionate, a kiss that left her clinging to him. When at last he lifted his head, he grinned down at her—a true smile, both dimples on display.

"Come home with me, my love?" he asked.

She smiled back at him, Mr. Devereaux Winter, the man she loved. "Yes."

EPILOGUE

$\mathcal{E}$milia was in the midst of finalizing her guest list for the country house party she and Dev would be holding at Abingdon House. The journey to Oxfordshire would not prove too treacherous in December, she hoped. The prospect of a party being held by the newly reformed Wicked Winter ought to prove plenty of allure, for the favorite *on dit* in Town was how the infamously reviled merchant had somehow found himself being embraced by society.

Over the last few months, she and Dev had worked hard to earn their place. Using her connections and friends as *entrée*, they had attended nearly every important social event they could. The scandal and scorn surrounding his name had begun to fade in the face of the united front they presented.

All London was agog with the notion of Mr. Devereaux Winter in love.

Emilia smiled to herself, for she could not blame them. She too was agog with the knowledge her husband had given her his heart. That he loved her every bit as much as she loved him. Lady Merton could go to the devil for all Emilia cared, and she most certainly would not be on the guest list for the house party.

It was to be held over Christmas, a gay affair, she hoped, and an excellent opportunity for the Winter sisters to ease their foray into society. There would be opportunities aplenty for matchmaking. And it would be held at Abingdon House, a magnificent estate which would undoubtedly draw a fair number of acceptances on its own.

Dev had recently purchased the property from her father at a fair price. He was also looking after Papa's finances, along with employing Mr. Rhodes, to make certain Papa would not be taken advantage of again. And for his part, having a companion to keep his mind from growing too idle seemed to have offset some of her father's confusion.

There was no cure for the illness that plagued him. Living next door enabled her to visit frequently, however. Dev often accompanied her, and the unexpected bond he had developed with her father warmed her heart each time she saw it. Mama too had become quite taken with Dev, who made certain to provide her and all her friends with an unlimited supply of his new Winters Soap.

Of course, his caring and consideration for her parents was not the only thing about her husband that warmed Emilia's heart.

Her smile deepened, accompanied by a swift rush of warmth. Her heart had not died with James, and in Dev's arms, she had rediscovered the healing power of love. She had also made peace with the knowledge that loving Dev did not in any way diminish her love for James. James would forever be the first man she had loved, and she would always treasure her memories of him.

But Dev was her husband, the man who shared her bed each night, the man who kissed her lips so sweetly and made love to her with such passionate tenderness. He had allowed her to finally accept that loving him was not a betrayal of James's memory, but rather another means of honoring it, of taking the love he had shown her and allowing it to blossom and grow.

Oh, how it had grown. And soon, it would grow even larger. The Winter family was about to grow in numbers by one more. But that was a secret she would reveal to her husband later. For now, she had a house party to attend to, she reminded herself sternly, for invitations would need to be issued, and she must make them with great care. No more woolgathering.

The futures of the Winter sisters could depend upon her choices. It was not ordinarily done for five sisters to enter society at once, but Dev had been hopelessly unaware of that before Emilia had entered his life, and it was too late to undo what had already been done. Which meant all five Winter ladies were about to go husband hunting.

Frowning, she scratched a name—the Earl of Knightley—from her list. He was far too dour to be a match for the Winter sisters. What had she been thinking? Emilia dipped her quill in ink as she thought of another potential suitor to add, the Earl of Hertford, who, while notoriously proper, was also pockets to let and in need of a wealthy bride.

Suddenly, the door adjoining her chamber to her husband's opened. She glanced up from her handsome writing desk to find Dev striding toward her, debonair in a pair of fawn breeches which hugged his muscular thighs to perfection and a dark coat and waistcoat. The cravat at his neck had been arranged into a simple mail coach knot, and yet he was more elegant than any duke she had ever seen.

She dropped her pen into her inkwell and stood, forgetting the necessity of her list at once in favor of her beloved.

"Mr. Winter," she greeted him formally, dipping into a curtsy as she drank in the sight of her handsome husband prowling toward her. There was something about the pretense of formality that heightened her awareness of him. "I was not expecting you so soon."

It was midafternoon, his sisters were learning new dance steps under the watchful eyes of their dance master and chaperone. Her new state had left her unaccountably tired. And hungry. Before settling in for her duties, she had donned a wrapper and taken a nap. She was still wearing the wrapper now, which she supposed had rendered her curtsy rather foolish.

Dev did not seem to mind. His dark gaze devoured her from head to toe as he bowed deeply. "My darling Mrs. Winter. Do you see how you are making a complete gentleman of me at last?"

The smile that was never far from her lips reemerged. "Pray do not become too much of a gentleman, sir. I love you just as you are."

He closed the remainder of the distance between them, and that was when she realized he held an oblong disc in his hand. "Never fear, darling. I am still just as much of a scoundrel as I have always been. If you require evidence, I shall be more than happy to provide it."

"Evidence?" She slid her arms around his neck, rising on her toes to press her mouth to his. The kiss deepened instantly, their tongues moving against each other. Hunger surged through her, an answering heat and burgeoning ache between her thighs.

"Mmm," he murmured into her mouth. One of his hands settled upon her waist in a possessive grasp. He kissed her slowly, lingeringly, as if he could not get enough of her. He kissed her as if he had spent all the hours since they had parted that morning desperately longing for her.

The sweet languor of desire slithered over her, invading every part of her body. Even her mind. Dev consumed her senses: he was all she breathed, all she saw, all she felt, all she tasted, the deep growl of satisfaction rumbling from his chest all she heard.

He withdrew his lips at last, staring down at her with enough naked devotion to rob her breath all over again. "I missed you, darling."

"It has only been a few hours since we last saw each other," she protested on a smile, even though she enjoyed the thought of her powerful husband harboring a weakness for her. "How could you have missed me already?"

He kissed her nose. "How could I not? Christ, woman." His lips found her cheek, her ear. "I missed your sweet skin." He dragged his mouth down her neck, sucking and nibbling as he went. "I missed the way you tremble in my arms, the way you kiss me, the way you wrap your arms around me."

"Oh." She could not seem to find anything more intelligent to say, because her husband was nibbling on her collarbone. "I missed you too, my love."

"Damnation, I love you." The hand gripping her waist left her to untie the knot on her robe.

Beneath it, she was naked, but she had no wish to stop him. She had no shame when it came to this man and her reaction to him. "And I love you." Her hands shifted, traveling over his broad shoulders, down his muscled arms. Such delicious strength his finery encompassed, and she wanted it gone. All gone.

No more barriers between them.

It did not signify that it was the midst of the day. Or that she had a house party the likes of which she had never even attended, let alone organized, to continue planning. Or that it was quite scandalous to make love to her husband whilst the sun was high in the London sky.

She had to have him.

All of him.

Now.

She worked his jacket from his shoulders, peeling it down his arms. It fell to the carpet with a soft thud. His cravat was next, her nimble fingers making quick work of the simple knot. Then his waistcoat.

"Bloody hell, I almost forgot. The soap," Dev said. "Your new blend has been created. I brought it home to get your opinion of the initial batch, and then I saw you...Lord, you're beautiful. Have I ever told you that?"

She kissed him. A quick peck of adoration, over before she could be tempted to prolong it. "A time or two, perhaps. But you may say so again anytime."

"You're beautiful." He kissed her again. "Your opinion on your soap, if you please. If I am whiling away the day in my wife's bed, at least I will have something to take back to my factory tomorrow."

She raised a brow, the heat swirling within her heightening. "In my bed? The entire day? I do like the sound of that, Mr. Winter."

"As do I." He held the bar of soap to her nose. "Smell, darling."

She inhaled dutifully. "It is divine, Dev." And just what she had suggested. "Cassia, jasmine, and lavender, with a hint of rose. Perfection."

"*You* are perfection." He grinned down at her before tossing the bar over his shoulder. "To the devil with the soap. Right now, all I care about is making love to my wife."

The guest list could wait, she decided, for a few hours at least.

They kissed again.

Or until tomorrow.

Dear God, how she loved this man.

* * *

Dev was desperately in love with his wife, and just when he thought he could not love her any more, the sun rose on another day. She made a soft sigh of contentment into his mouth as he deepened their kiss. His left hand sank into the thick, silken strands of her hair. Though her lustrous brown locks had been swept into a neat chignon by her lady's maid, his fingers were already locating pins and plucking them.

They dropped to the floor, one by one.

His right hand finished working on the remnants of the knot keeping her dressing gown in place. It opened, and he wasted no time in pulling the bloody thing off whilst he ravished her mouth. The last of her pins fell away, and her long hair tumbled down her back. Warm, smooth feminine curves met his hand.

He was insatiable when it came to Emilia.

Never breaking their kiss, he moved them to her bed. They reached it, and he tore his mouth from hers at last to rain kisses down her throat, over her breasts, to her nipples. He could not resist sucking one of the sweet pink peaks into his mouth, then flicking his tongue over it until she moaned.

His fingers dipped into her folds, and she was slick and hot.

He hummed his approval as he suckled her other breast next. "You are so wet for me, my love. Tell me, do you want me?"

Her hips were already moving against his hand, seeking more. "I need you inside me, Dev."

Her throaty words proved his undoing. A rush of lust so potent it nearly brought him to his knees arrowed straight to his cock. He circled her pearl, then slid his touch lower. Her cunny was dripping. He sank two fingers deep inside, curling them toward him. She clenched, gripping him, and his cock twitched in response.

"Do you need me like this, darling?" he asked, enjoying teasing her.

She moaned as he brushed his thumb over her clitoris. "Yes. But more."

Dev was not a man who resisted a challenge. He was more than happy to give her more. He kissed down her belly and sank to his knees before her. His fingers still inside her, he replaced his thumb with his tongue. Dev licked her, then sucked, fucking her in slow and steady strokes as he tortured her with his tongue and teeth.

She grasped his hair, arching into him and thrusting herself against his face. He was greedy for her, so damned greedy. He wanted her to come on his tongue. To lick her until she shuddered against him and found her release. She tasted so good, and the seductive sounds in her throat were enough to make his cock painfully rigid in his breeches.

When she spent, it was almost violent. She clamped on his fingers, spasms rocking through her as she cried out, her knees buckling. He pinned her to the bed with his free hand, keeping her from toppling over as he continued flicking his tongue over her pearl.

"Oh, Dev," she gasped.

He smiled against her, then kissed her before sinking back on his haunches. "You're bloody beautiful, Emilia. I could watch you like this forever."

He withdrew his fingers and then plunged them back into her. From this angle, he could see the glistening pink of her flesh, the place where he entered her. Desire hit him, potent and fierce. If he was not inside her soon, he would spend in his breeches instead of inside her.

Reluctantly, he withdrew, and then, meeting her gaze, sucked her wetness from his fingers. Her pupils were dark and large in eyes glazed with passion. "Sweet, too," he said. "So sweet."

"Now, Dev," she murmured. "I cannot wait."

Emilia grasped handfuls of his shirt and tugged him to his feet, then helped him to haul it over his head. They moved to the fall of his breeches next as he toed off his shoes. His stockings and breeches were whipped away by both of them, and naked and kissing each other, they fell upon the bed.

He was on his back, Emilia atop him, his hands buried in the silken curtain of her hair, tongue in her mouth. She broke the kiss to trail more down his neck, across his chest, all the way to his navel.

He groaned. "Emilia, do not."

If she took him in her mouth, he would not last, and he had every intention of losing himself inside her cunny.

"I want to taste you," she said, glancing up at him wickedly as she kissed below his navel.

"Emilia—"

All further protest was cut short by his wife's tongue flicking over the head of his cock. His ability to think fled. She swirled her tongue over him in leisurely exploration, licking a drop leaking from the tip.

"Mmm," was all she said, and then she sucked him deep into her mouth.

He could not fight the instinct to move. His hips jerked, and she took him down her throat. An incoherent string of profanity unleashed from him. She began a rhythm, moving up and down his shaft. The sight of his engorged prick disappearing between her lips was enough to make his ballocks tighten.

"Damn it," he growled, somehow finding the Herculean strength to stop her before he spent. "I want to be inside you when I come."

Her lips were swollen and glistening as he rolled her to

her back and settled between her thighs. He covered her mouth with his as he aligned himself with her center. One hard thrust, and he was inside her. They sighed in unison as he moved, pumping his hips in fast, hard thrusts.

She was so hot, so tight. With his tongue in her mouth, he reached between them to work her pearl. She bucked against him, nipping his lower lip. *Damn*, but he loved it when she was ravenous for him. He felt the same way. He drove into her again, angling her hips to deepen his penetration. Her juices coated his cock, dripping down his ballocks, and still he rammed into her.

He could not stop.

On a strangled cry, she came again, her body tensing beneath his. Her cunny contracted, milking him, and a burst of desire rolled down his spine. He was going to lose control in another moment. One more savage thrust, and he joined his wife in oblivion, emptying himself deep inside her womb.

For an indeterminate span of time, he remained as he was, inside her, their hearts pounding together. He feathered soft kisses over her mouth, over her cheeks, her nose. "I can see I shall have to make a habit of bringing you soap," he said, gazing down at her with all the love bursting in his heart.

She smiled back at him, framing his face with her hands. "There is something I must tell you, Dev."

He kissed the tip of her nose once more. "What is it, sweet?"

"You are going to be a father."

Emotion rocked through him. He searched her gaze. "Emilia? You are…?"

She nodded, giving him a shy look. "I am with child. Does it please you?"

Holy. God.

Did it please him? Shock gave way to sheer joy.

"Hell yes, it pleases me. A child." His hand crept to the

gentle swell of her belly, cradling it reverently. "I could not be happier, my darling. Are *you* happy? Are you well?"

Good Lord, he had just been a rutting beast.

"I have never been happier," she assured him, drawing his head down to hers for a slow kiss.

That turned into another kiss.

And another.

When at last he lifted his head, he was breathless, filled with contentment, and hardening inside her, ready to make love to her all over again. "Perhaps I can make you even happier," he teased.

"I am certain you can, my wicked man," she told him, wrapping her legs around his waist.

"I will do my very best, Mrs. Winter." He grinned against her lips.

Life, he decided, was damned good.

Now all he had to do was see his sisters as happy as he was…

The End.

AUTHOR'S NOTE

$\mathcal{T}$hank you for reading *Wicked in Winter*! I hope you enjoyed this first book in my The Wicked Winters series and that Dev and Emilia's story touched your heart. From the moment Devereaux Winter and his sisters first appeared in my mind, I knew I had to write their stories. All of them.

As always, please consider leaving an honest review of *Wicked in Winter*. Reviews are greatly appreciated! If you'd like to keep up to date with my latest releases and series news, sign up for my newsletter here or follow me on Amazon or BookBub. Join my reader's group on Facebook for bonus content, early excerpts, giveaways, and more.

If you'd like a preview of *Wedded in Winter*, Book Two in The Wicked Winters, do read on.

Until next time,
Scarlett

PREVIEW OF WEDDED IN WINTER

Beatrix Winter has no wish to marry any of the lords her brother has in mind for her. There is only one man she has ever desired, but as her overbearing brother's loyal right-hand man, Merrick Hart has never spared her a glance. When the entire Winter family departs to celebrate Christmas in the country, unintentionally leaving Beatrix behind, Merrick reluctantly agrees to escort her to her brother's estate. But despite the winter's unusual cold, their journey quickly becomes heated. Beatrix is the one temptation Merrick has always managed to resist, but a man can only endure so much time alone with the woman he has been secretly longing for before he takes what he wants…

* * *

Chapter One
London, 1813

Bea descended from her hired hack, weary to her bones and in desperate need of sleep and a bath. Or perhaps rather a bath first, and then sleep. She had been awake all night long, and her mind was as bleary as her vision. With great effort, she had remained reasonably lucid on her way home. She had her pistol in her reticule as always, but she was a Winter, and no one knew better than she just how cruel the world could be.

Now, at last, with Dudley House before her, her bed within the reach of footsteps rather than a chilled hackney ride, she could relax. A blustery burst of early December air buffeted her cheeks and caught her dress like a sail as she made her way to the entrance. For the last two months, she had been escaping the notice of her stern older brother Dev, coming and going as she pleased by slipping out and then back in when the servants and her boisterous family members were otherwise occupied.

This time, however, unease gripped her as she hastily fitted the key she had thieved from the housekeeper into the lock. She had never been gone all through the night before. She only hoped her brother had not noticed her absence at breakfast. Since he had married his wife, Lady Emilia, Dev had been blissfully distracted.

The lock clicked, and, holding her breath, she slipped inside. Nary a butler, a maid, or a footman was anywhere to be seen, and the entire house was strangely silent. She paused for a moment in the marbled entryway as she listened for sounds.

Still, nothing but the thudding of her heart.

There was something distinctly ominous about the hush.

It seemed odd indeed, for her four older sisters, while beloved, were—there was no other way to politely describe them—as noisy as a henhouse. Frowning, she made her way slowly through the entrance hall, determined to seek the staircase and race up it with all haste.

But just as she passed the library, the door opened.

"I beg your pardon, madam," called out a deep, masculine voice she recognized all too well. "Where do you think you are going?"

Want more? Get *Wedded in Winter* now!

DON'T MISS SCARLETT'S OTHER ROMANCES!

Complete Book List
HISTORICAL ROMANCE

Heart's Temptation
A Mad Passion (Book One)
Rebel Love (Book Two)
Reckless Need (Book Three)
Sweet Scandal (Book Four)
Restless Rake (Book Five)
Darling Duke (Book Six)
The Night Before Scandal (Book Seven)

Wicked Husbands
Her Errant Earl (Book One)
Her Lovestruck Lord (Book Two)
Her Reformed Rake (Book Three)
Her Deceptive Duke (Book Four)
Her Missing Marquess (Book Five)
Her Virtuous Viscount (Book Six)

League of Dukes
Nobody's Duke (Book One)
Heartless Duke (Book Two)
Dangerous Duke (Book Three)
Shameless Duke (Book Four)
Scandalous Duke (Book Five)
Fearless Duke (Book Six)

Notorious Ladies of London
Lady Ruthless (Book One)
Lady Wallflower (Book Two)
Lady Reckless (Book Three)
Lady Wicked (Book Four)
Lady Lawless (Book Five)

The Wicked Winters
Wicked in Winter (Book One)
Wedded in Winter (Book Two)
Wanton in Winter (Book Three)
Wishes in Winter (Book 3.5)
Willful in Winter (Book Four)
Wagered in Winter (Book Five)
Wild in Winter (Book Six)
Wooed in Winter (Book Seven)
Winter's Wallflower (Book Eight)
Winter's Woman (Book Nine)
Winter's Whispers (Book Ten)
Winter's Waltz (Book Eleven)
Winter's Widow (Book Twelve)
Winter's Warrior (Book Thirteen)

The Sinful Suttons
Sutton's Spinster (Book One)

Stand-alone Novella
Lord of Pirates

CONTEMPORARY ROMANCE
Love's Second Chance
Reprieve (Book One)
Perfect Persuasion (Book Two)
Win My Love (Book Three)

Coastal Heat
Loved Up (Book One)

ABOUT THE AUTHOR

USA Today and Amazon bestselling author Scarlett Scott writes steamy Victorian and Regency romance with strong, intelligent heroines and sexy alpha heroes. She lives in Pennsylvania and Maryland with her Canadian husband, adorable identical twins, and one TV-loving dog.

A self-professed literary junkie and nerd, she loves reading anything, but especially romance novels, poetry, and Middle English verse. Catch up with her on her website http://www.scarlettscottauthor.com/. Hearing from readers never fails to make her day.

Scarlett's complete book list and information about upcoming releases can be found at http://www.scarlettscottauthor.com/.

Connect with Scarlett! You can find her here:
    Join Scarlett Scott's reader's group on Facebook for early excerpts, giveaways, and a whole lot of fun!
    Sign up for her newsletter here.
    Follow Scarlett on Amazon
    Follow Scarlett on BookBub
    www.instagram.com/scarlettscottauthor/
    www.twitter.com/scarscoromance
    www.pinterest.com/scarlettscott
    www.facebook.com/AuthorScarlettScott

Made in the USA
Monee, IL
29 October 2021